# JAKE ATLAS

## AND THE KEYS OF THE APOCALYPSE

*Other books by Rob Lloyd Jones*

*Jake Atlas and the Tomb of the Emerald Snake*

*Jake Atlas and the Hunt for the Feathered God*

*Jake Atlas and the Quest for the Crystal Mountain*

*Wild Boy*

*Wild Boy and the Black Terror*

# JAKE ATLAS
## AND THE KEYS OF THE APOCALYPSE

ROB LLOYD JONES

WALKER BOOKS

This is a work of fiction. Names, characters, places and incidents are either the product of the author's imagination or, if real, used fictitiously. All statements, activities, stunts, descriptions, information and material of any other kind contained herein are included for entertainment purposes only and should not be relied on for accuracy or replicated as they may result in injury.

First published 2020 by Walker Books Ltd
87 Vauxhall Walk, London SE11 5HJ

2 4 6 8 10 9 7 5 3 1


Cover illustration by Petur Antonsson



This book has been typeset in TC Veljovic

Printed and bound by CPI Group (UK) Ltd, Croydon CR0 4YY



British Library Cataloguing in Publication Data
A catalogue record for this book is available from the British Library

ISBN 978-1-4063-8501-4

www.walker.co.uk

*To Mara, editor extraordinaire,*
*who kept Jake safe throughout his adventures*

# 1

"To save the world, you must first save yourself."

Mum nodded thoughtfully.

Dad nodded even more thoughtfully.

My twin sister, Pan, nodded so thoughtfully it was like her head had gone into slow motion. It was as if this was the most profound thing any of them had ever heard.

I stared at them, and then at the old man by the fire who had spoken.

"What does that even mean?" I asked.

The wise man grinned at me, showing off rows of brown teeth and black gums. He beckoned me closer with a finger that looked like a Twiglet.

"He who lacks knowledge often knows too much," he rasped.

"Oh, come on," I replied. "That's even more meaningless."

I stared at my family, who were gathered cross-legged around the pulsing embers. They'd been spellbound by every bit of nonsense this old guy had croaked.

"Why are you all nodding?" I asked. "It's gibberish."

"Just sit and listen, Jake," Mum hissed.

I didn't want to sit, or to listen to any more of this stuff. The old man could say whatever he wanted – it was his temple, after all – but I'd heard it before, from the dozen other "old wise men" we'd visited in the past month. We'd sought their help decoding symbols on an ancient relic, but they'd just confused us even more.

I gestured to the artefact, a small wooden box that trembled in the old guy's shaky hands. It was about the size of a Rubik's Cube, and carved all over with symbols that neither of my parents – both experts in ancient languages – or my sister, who is a weird genius, recognized.

"Have you seen anything like this before?" I asked.

He flashed me another goofy, black and brown smile. "He who truly sees has no need to see."

I groaned, and turned to stare out of the temple window. We were in Kathmandu, Nepal, doing *archaeology*. My parents were training me and my twin sister to be treasure hunters. Mum and Dad had spent a decade hunting for lost relics around the world, to stop them being sold on the black market. They'd been the best in the business, and maybe still were. But before *that* they were archaeologists, which is not so cool.

Treasure hunting is all excitement and rushing around. Usually, bad guys are after the same thing, so we have to get there first. But archaeology is slow.

So slow.

Did you know that after Howard Carter found Tutankhamen's tomb it took him ten years to remove all the treasure? Painstakingly recording every item, wrapping each artefact...

Finding the tomb was treasure hunting. Taking out the loot? Archaeology. I'd have had all of that stuff out in a day.

Four weeks ago we found a box. It had been hidden in Tibet by a civilization that existed before Ancient Egypt but was mysteriously wiped out. Its survivors had left clues in their tombs, which led us to this box. We feared that whatever disaster destroyed them might come again and kill millions. Maybe the box contained information to stop it from happening. That sounds urgent, right?

But the box had become *archaeology*.

Here's a version of an argument we'd had about fifty times over the past few weeks:

"We can't just open it, Jake," Mum insisted. "It's not that simple."

"It is! It's a box. I open boxes all the time. I opened one the other day. If you just hand it over, I'll—"

"Did the box you opened have the potential to

unleash a force that will wipe out all civilization?"

"Depends what you think of Cornflakes."

"Well *this* isn't a Cornflake box, Jake. We have no idea what it is. It could be a weapon, or a trap. Opening it could be exactly what the lost civilization wanted."

"Mum, I think they were trying to help us. They wanted to protect us against whatever destroyed them."

"We don't know that, Jake. That's why we have to study this long and hard before we open it."

"How long and how hard? Because I would say three weeks is longer and harder than any box needs to be—"

"Howard Carter spent ten years studying Tutankhamen's tomb before—"

"I know, Mum! But maybe he could have spent one year doing that, and nine finding other tombs."

"Jake, we have time to study this. It's our responsibility as archaeologists."

"We're treasure hunters!"

"There shouldn't be a difference."

"Of course there is! Treasure hunters open boxes, archaeologists talk about them."

Part of me knew Mum was right. The bad guys I mentioned were part of an evil organization we called the People of the Snake. They wanted to keep the lost civilization, and its fate, secret. They feared mass panic if people found out the world might end, but we felt people deserved to know. We'd succeeded in finding the box before they did, and were hiding out in Nepal. For once we did have time. But, well...

"Argh!" I groaned.

For the hundredth time, I considered grabbing the box and smashing it open. Light from the fire flickered off its carvings. Each side was decorated with a symbol of a snake curled in a circle, eating its own tail. We'd seen that sign a lot over the past year. It was painted on the walls of the lost civilization's tombs, and engraved on their crystal coffins.

The box was carved from a single piece of wood. It had no lid, but something was inside. Each time we tilted it we heard a hollow *thunk*. We didn't even know what sort of wood the box was carved from. We'd tried to have it analyzed, but it wasn't from any known tree.

"Come closer, come closer."

The wise man waggled a bony finger over one side of the box. "See here," he rasped. "This symbol. It is called an ouroboros."

"We know it recurs across ancient cultures," Dad added. "It's carved on Egyptian temples, tombs in the Indus Valley, and appears in Sumerian and Ancient Greek documents."

"It symbolizes renewal," Mum explained, "possibly in reference to the cycle of the seasons."

"No," the wise man wheezed. "Not a cycle of renewal. A cycle of *destruction*."

He held the box closer to the fire to study the

carving in the glimmering light. He was still grinning, but there was something different about his smile. It looked forced, trembling at the edges. A grimace more than a grin.

"Yes," he repeated. "A cycle of destruction."

Mum nodded slowly – she knew the guy was guessing but she was going along with it to be polite. But Dad's reaction was different. He grabbed the box from the old guy, glaring at it, and drew such a sharp breath that his glasses fell off. He snatched them up and shot Mum *such* a disapproving look, his forehead wrinkling and his bushy eyebrows sinking so low they looked like they were trying to wriggle down his nose.

I'd become quite good at deciphering my parents' silent conversations and secret signals, but this was something new. Usually Mum disapproved of anything dangerous, Dad tried to convince her that maybe it wasn't *so* dangerous, and then Mum told him that it was and that the conversation was over – all in eye signals, tilts of heads and puffs of cheeks.

But that had changed since our visit to Tibet. *Dad* had changed.

Now, he was the cautious one – scared, even. I knew why. We all did, even though none of us ever mentioned it.

In Tibet, I'd been separated from my family in an avalanche. For a short time they thought I'd died, and it had really affected Dad. We'd been in dangerous situations before – loads – but those few days in

Tibet had made him realize just *how* dangerous this could get. Of course I *hadn't* died – I'd trekked across the Himalayas to beat the People of the Snake to the box – but it seemed as if that last adventure had put out a fire in Dad. I'd heard him argue with Mum when they thought we were asleep, insisting that we should abandon this quest and return home to England.

Mum might have agreed a few months ago, but she had changed too, in a different way. Until Tibet she'd never properly believed in the lost civilization or that there was *really* a serious threat to the whole world. She'd often called the whole idea "mumbo jumbo". Now that she knew it was true, she was determined to follow this clue to wherever it led.

Just ... really slowly.

"I think it's time we let someone else deal with this," Dad muttered, staring at the box.

"No, John," Mum disagreed, "we just need to be cautious."

I groaned. That meant another month of study, at least.

"How about X-raying it?" I suggested. "At least we could get a hint of what's inside."

"We've spoken about that, Jake," Mum reminded me. "We don't know what harm it might do to the contents."

"But we'd have a clue to what's in there," I persisted. "That'd be more than we've found out from a dozen old wise men."

What happened next surprised me. Mum sighed, very heavily, and looked at Dad.

"Maybe Jake's right, John?"

"Remember!" the wise man hissed. "He who is right is not always wise."

"Oh, stop," I mumbled under my breath. "I say we should vote on it. More crazy wise men, or an X-ray? Hands up for an X-ray."

Mum glanced at Dad again. Then, a little reluctantly, she raised her hand. Pan grinned and did the same.

"All right!" I declared. "Three against one."

Dad handed Mum the box. "An X-ray," he agreed. "Nothing more."

The wise man offered a few other meaningless comments as we packed our bags and thanked him for his help. As we left the temple and stepped back into the dazzling Nepalese sunlight, he called out one last time.

"Boy!"

I turned, happy to let him have the final word; after all, this was his home, and we had sought his help. I had no idea that, of all his seemingly nonsensical predictions, this last one would turn out to be spot on.

"The cycle of destruction," he said, "has begun."

# 2

There must have been a million pigeons in the square outside the temple, and each had pooed at least ten times. The birds were thick on the temple roofs, perched on wood carvings around the eaves, and squashed together on the heads of Hindu gods that stood in alcoves around the square. Hundreds of them flapped into the air, all feathers and squawks, as we marched from the wise man's temple.

We were in Durbar Square, a temple precinct at the heart of Kathmandu, and we were in disguise. Most tourists came to Nepal to trek in the mountains, so we'd bought hiking gear – walking boots and trousers with loads of pointless pockets – and matching rucksacks, as if we were about to set off on an expedition to Everest.

I didn't think it mattered; the people who were pursuing us wouldn't be fooled by disguises. For starters, Pan always dressed as a Goth, with raven-dyed hair, black lipstick and a black hoodie that she wore no matter how hot it was or how much she stuck out like a sore thumb. And if the People of the Snake suspected we were in Kathmandu, they'd scour the city with drones rigged with facial-recognition cameras and other high-tech gadgets.

But we had some fancy kit of our own. As we walked, Dad slid on what looked like a pair of wrap-around sunglasses, but which were actually wearable computers called smart-goggles. Microphones in their frames recognized his voice as he instructed the goggles to find the closest hospital with an X-ray machine.

"There's one a mile from here," he said.

"Maybe we can ask nicely," Pan replied.

We all laughed, except Dad. *Asking nicely* usually meant breaking in and not asking at all. We'd need a plan, blueprints of the hospital and schematics of the security cameras, but we were used to all that. It felt great to be *doing* something.

I'd miss Kathmandu. It was my kind of place: crazy and hectic. Walking among its streets was like playing a complicated game for which you were never told the rules. Everyone else seemed to know where to go and what to do. Not that they were getting anywhere. The maze-like lanes were jammed with bikes, pedicabs, carts. Drivers cursed each other, each convinced they had the right of way. Noises rang from every direction: street sellers and dogs barking, scooter engines and chanting monks, warning bells from pedicabs and urgent taxi horns. The air was so thick with dust and diesel fumes that even the locals wore paper masks or pulled scarves up over their faces.

Many of the buildings were still damaged from an earthquake that ravaged the city several years ago. Cracks in walls were so wide that you could see into buildings. Wavy grass grew up where roofs had collapsed, as if the houses had sprouted hair. But everywhere you looked there were splashes of colour. Litter-strewn alleys led to spotless sunny courtyards. Concrete towers parted to reveal Hindu temples with intricate wood carvings or Buddhist stupas painted like rainbows. Women wore bright orange saris, red and gold slippers and jangling arrays of jewellery. I loved places like this, where not everything was nice, but nothing was ever dull. It felt *alive*.

"Stick together," Dad called.

He led the way through the chaos, weaving between a stall selling pomegranates and watermelons and a small shrine on which candles dribbled wax down the faces of stone gods. We always moved fast. Our eyes darted around the street, watching for danger. This time, though, mine lingered a little longer on each sight. We'd be moving on soon, so I wanted to enjoy these moments. An old man in a doorway flogged pots and pans. An even older woman sold flower garlands for a festival. Sunburned tourists studied guidebooks, while an electrician on a ladder struggled to make sense of a knot of power cables that–

I stopped.

I stood among the bustle, staring at the man on the ladder.

An alarm went off in my head, an instinct I'd come to trust. Slowly, I pulled my smart-goggles from my backpack and slid them on.

"We're blown," I whispered.

My family, who were wearing their goggles too, stopped.

"What do you see?" Mum asked.

It might sound weird that Mum – one of the best treasure hunters ever – was asking me what I saw. I have this strange way of spotting patterns among chaos, of thinking fast and turning plans into action. Where others stopped, I moved. And when they moved, I often stopped and stared. I didn't know *what* I had seen, just that something wasn't right.

That guy up the ladder...

I'd seen plenty of electricians in Kathmandu, fiddling with tangles of cables that crisscrossed over the streets. Most wore the same green overalls, faded and dirty. But this guy's overalls were spotless, with fold creases, as if brand new. Maybe they were – or maybe he wasn't really an electrician.

"I think we're being watched," I said.

"Then we should assume we are," Mum replied.

"We need to split up," I added.

"No, we should definitely not split up," Dad insisted.

"We all have identical rucksacks," I protested. "They can't know which of us has the box. If they catch us together, they'll get it for sure. If we split up, we may keep it from them."

"Unless they have enough mercenaries to follow us all," Pan noted.

That was possible. The People of the Snake used hired goons, ex-military thugs, to do their dirty work. We'd encountered heaps of them; they seemed on endless supply. Usually they wore black combat suits, like Special Forces soldiers, and were kitted out with smart-goggles and utility belts packed with gadgets. But they loved a disguise too.

"I agree with Jake," Mum decided. It was the second time she'd said that this morning, and I hadn't got used to it.

"You do?" I asked.

"Four streets run off this junction. Take one each and meet back at the hotel."

On the ladder, the electrician continued to fiddle with the cables. Maybe I was being paranoid. We'd been out of action for two months; I was out of practice. But there was something I hadn't told my family. I'd switched bags with Mum when we left the temple.

I had the box.

I'd found the artefact in Tibet, but had barely been allowed to touch it since. It was childish of me, but I just wanted to carry it for a bit. But Mum was a trained fighter; she had a far better chance of holding on to the thing if it came to a scrap.

I should have said something, but I was terrified of owning up. We didn't know for sure that anyone was following us. By the time I got back to the hotel, my parents would be so relieved I was OK that they'd forget I'd switched bags.

I hoped.

"OK," Mum said, "see you at the hotel."

And we all left.

I set off again through the bustle, gripping the strap of my backpack in case anyone tried to snatch it. I was heading for a square that looked busy. Chants and songs echoed around its tall buildings, and a cloud of red smoke drifted over a thick crowd. It looked like a festival. Could I even get through?

*"Rear view,"* I whispered.

The scene in my lenses changed, as reverse cameras in the goggles' frames showed the street behind me. My heart stopped, and then started going double speed.

The electrician was coming after me.

Clean overalls turned dirty as he splashed through a puddle. His face was hidden beneath a baseball cap, but I saw him touch his ear, listening to an order in his comms bud. There was no doubt: we'd been found.

I barged my way into the crowd. I had no idea what festival I'd stumbled into, but it was popular. Across the square, a group of men pushed a wooden cart as big as a minibus, carrying what looked like a fifty-foot Christmas tree, with ribbons around every branch and a flag fluttering at its top. The cart – and tree – trundled slowly through the crowd as people banged drums, clanged cymbals and hurled flowers into its path.

The drumming grew faster, seeming to keep time with my heart as I forced my way closer to the cart. I had a history of doing crazy stunts against these mercenaries; they'd expect me to cause chaos to aid my escape – probably to knock over that giant tree. They would be directing back-up teams towards the cart, laying a trap...

I turned and barged through in the other direction, away from the cart. The crowd pushed against me, but I elbowed and wriggled, squeezing into a market at the other side of the square. As I rushed between stalls laid with piles of brightly coloured spices, I was buzzing. My parents had trained me to be less impulsive, to think *smarter*, not just faster. I'd done exactly that, out-thinking the People of the Snake and protecting the—

Ahead, two Western women blocked the path between the stalls. They glared at me, and one of them touched her ear.

*Oh, God...*

I turned down a different aisle, but another mercenary was blocking it. Now there were seven of them advancing between the stalls. Each had an arm pressed against their side, concealing a weapon under their coat. That was even worse news. Usually these guys carried electrolaser stun guns that fired fizzing bolts of electricity easily powerful enough to knock out a giant, let alone little old me.

I hid behind a spice stall, wishing I *had* knocked over that tree. I was trapped like a rat, as mercenaries stalked me from every direction. I dumped my backpack down and yanked out the box. I was going to be caught, but not until I knew what was inside this thing...

I picked up a brick and slammed it against the side of the box. The wood didn't even crack. I hit it harder, again and again, cursing with each strike. I needed something stronger, something like...

I jumped up from behind the stall.

"Hey!" I yelled. "Over here!"

One of the mercenaries pulled out his stun gun, a silver handgun with a crab claw-shaped barrel. A ball of blue light gathered in the crab claw, and a lightning bolt of electricity fired at me. I dropped back to the ground, tossing the box in the air so the shot hit the relic. I covered my head with my arms as shattered wood showered my back.

Something else hit me, too.

Something from inside the box.

I scrambled around, eyes stinging from spices blown up from the stalls. A round object lay beside me. I grabbed it, struggling to see. It was made of crystal and was the shape of a pocket watch, although twice the size. One side was engraved with the ouroborus symbol of the snake eating its tail. The other was made up of hundreds of crystal cogs, like the inside of a watch. Some of the cogs were so tiny I could barely see them.

"Jake Atlas!" one of the mercenaries barked. "Give us the box."

"You just blew it up!" I cried.

"Give us the device."

Device? That was a strange word. Devices *do things*. The more I stared at the artefact, the more I sensed that it wasn't *just* an artefact. It felt *powerful.*

With a shaky finger, I turned one of the cogs. Even above the noise of the festival, the shouts from the mercenaries and the screams of fleeing shoppers in the market, I swear I heard the cog move – three soft clicks that caused every other cog to turn too. *Click click click.*

Nothing happened. I don't know what I expected – this thing was thousands of years old; of course it didn't work.

And my time was up.

Fear rose like sick in my throat. They'd easily overpower me, but maybe I could get in a couple of punches first. But my hands were shaking with fear.

Hang on.

It wasn't fear.

It was the device.

It was trembling slightly, like a smartphone set to vibrate. As I held it closer, a drop of sweat fell from my forehead and onto the dials. I sensed that it was about to ... well, to do *something*. But then it stopped.

And now something *else* was shaking.

I rose a fraction and turned, confused. The stall I was hiding behind had begun to rattle. Then the next one did too, and the next, a shudder spreading across the market. One of the tables jumped as if it had been kicked from below, tossing its spices into a multi-coloured cloud.

Was this another earthquake?

I scrambled back, coughing and rubbing my eyes. Behind me, another stall flipped over, and I leaped up in fright. I was exposed to the mercenaries' weapons, but they weren't looking at me anymore. They'd turned to stare at the square; the buildings had started to shake, and cheers had turned into screams. Everyone ran, pushing and shoving. The tree swayed on its cart, then toppled over and crashed down across the ground.

The mercenaries yelled frantically at one another. This was my chance to escape. I shoved the device into my backpack and joined the stampede of people fleeing the square. One of the mercenaries yelled an order to find me, but I was already gone.

# 3

"Don't speak. Don't even open your mouth. Just nod or shake your head. Do you have the box?"

I nodded, then shook my head. It was a tricky question to answer. I couldn't help opening my mouth either, as I leaned against the hotel room wall gasping for breath. I'd foolishly expected my family to be happy, or at least relieved, to see me. Instead they glared as if they were competing to look the most furious.

"Where is the box?" Mum snapped.

I slid down the wall and sat on the carpet, wiping spice-scented sweat from my face. "I broke it open," I wheezed.

Pan bolted up from the bed. "You did *what?*"

"I had to. They were going to catch me. I only got away thanks to the earthquake."

"What earthquake?" Dad asked.

I looked at each member of my family, but their

faces were blank. Dad nudged his glasses up his nose. "Perhaps just a tremor," he suggested.

"No, it was huge," I insisted. "Buildings shook. A massive tree fell down."

After I'd escaped the mercenaries, I'd hidden in an alley near the square, catching my breath and calming my nerves. The earthquake had been brief, but no one in the streets beyond the square seemed aware it had even happened. There was no panic, no damage. Everything seemed normal.

*Was* it an earthquake?

"Here," I wheezed. "This was in the box."

I pulled the device from my backpack and, trembling, held it out. My family edged forward.

"What is it?" Pan asked.

"Don't know... Don't touch the cogs..."

"Jake, calm down," Mum insisted. "Tell us everything."

I explained what had happened. As I spoke, Dad mumbled about "unnecessary risks" and Pan muttered that the whole story sounded like a load of rubbish.

"It's true," I snapped. "That's what happened."

"Perhaps there was a gas leak under the square," Dad muttered, "or some sort of–"

"No, it was *this*."

I dumped the device on a side table and flopped onto the bed.

Dad glanced at Mum, who rolled her eyes. She

hadn't said my story was mumbo jumbo, but I knew she was thinking it.

Dad picked up the device. He was a historian, so he always handled relics with care, but this was different. He was acting like it was something he feared rather than respected.

"Which cog did you turn?" he asked.

"Don't touch *any*," I yelped.

Carefully, he turned the crystal device over and examined the snake symbol. "It could be an astrological mechanism. Archimedes created clock-like devices in Ancient Greece."

"Were they as complex as this?" Pan asked.

"No way near," Dad replied. "The cog system here is extraordinary."

"So what does it do?" Pan wondered. "Why did the lost civilization hide it, and how does it help us find out what happened to them?"

They were good questions, but there was only one thing I wanted to know.

"When can we get rid of it?" I asked.

Either they didn't hear or they chose to ignore me. Mum took the device from Dad, slid on her smart-goggles and instructed them to zoom to inspect the dials more closely.

"John, look at these," she said. "The way they interlock. Does that remind you of anything?"

"You're thinking of the Capitoline mechanism?" Dad guessed.

"What's that?" Pan asked.

Mum turned to a desk, and what looked like a large tablet computer. She tapped the screen in three spots, and holograms beamed from the glass, projecting web pages into the air. It was a 3D computer that we called a holosphere, from which we could search almost any archaeological report or museum archive in the world. It was pretty awesome for gaming too.

*"Show archive for the Capitoline Museums,"* Mum instructed.

"Capitoline Museums?" Pan asked. "In Rome?"

The holosphere projected a list of thousands of the museum's artefacts. Each was represented by a bullet point giving a name, a date and the place where the relic was found.

*"Filter to Roman collection,"* Mum said.

The hologram flickered, and the list reappeared with fewer entries. Using two fingers, Mum scrolled until she found what she was looking for. She pinched the bullet point and spread her fingers. The hologram changed to a pin-sharp 3D image of the artefact. Whatever it was was badly corroded, and encrusted with what looked like coral.

"What's that?" I asked.

"We're not sure," Dad replied. My parents often said "we" when they meant experts in general. "It was found in a shipwreck off the coast of Turkey," Dad continued. "The ship was Roman but, beyond that, no one knows much about this item."

"So why are we looking at it?" Pan asked.

Mum circled an area of the projection with her finger so that the image zoomed in on one of the few parts that wasn't covered in coral.

"Is that glass?" I asked.

"Crystal," Dad said.

"But the Romans didn't make crystal objects like this," Pan added.

"That's why it's such a mystery," Mum agreed. "X-rays have suggested this artefact has cogs, like clockwork."

"So you think this is the same thing as our device?" Pan asked.

"There's a similarity, that's all."

"But why would a Roman ship carry it?" I asked. "Our device was hidden by a civilization that came thousands of years *before* the Romans."

"I don't know, Jake," Mum said, with a sigh that suggested she was annoyed by the question. "We need to look at the Roman one more closely."

"How do we do that?" I persisted.

"We go to Rome."

# 4

Until a year ago, my only knowledge of the ancient world was about the Romans. My parents were experts in several ancient civilizations, but none of the others really registered with me. I'd seen *Gladiator*, and at school we learned about the Roman army. I liked the Romans; they didn't seem as complicated as the others. They were just like, "Hi, we're the Romans and we're going to take your land because we're tougher than you." I appreciated them for keeping things simple.

We flew to Rome using fake identities, and took a taxi to a hotel in the centre. Whenever we travelled somewhere new, we were always in a rush to follow some clue or other. Views from taxi windows were often our best chance to see a place, and this was one I didn't want to miss. Even Mum and Dad seemed in awe, staring in every direction as our cab carried us through the city's narrow lanes.

It was as if the whole city was a palace. Every flight of steps was lined with marble statues, and every roundabout was decorated with a fancy fountain with gods and heroes squirting water from bits of their bodies. Everything looked ancient to me, but Pan gleefully told me I was wrong. Some of the statues were from the Renaissance, when artists with the same names as Teenage Mutant Ninja Turtles copied Roman styles.

Actually, it wasn't all fancy. The grander the city, the tackier its shops – and Rome was as grand as cities got. Every other store was flogging cheap souvenirs. Some of the stuff had the Pope on it, but most was to do with Ancient Rome: Colosseum fridge magnets, mugs with Roman emperors giving a thumbs-up, cheap plastic gladiator helmets.

"Have you been here before?" I asked.

"Been?" Dad replied. "We used to live here."

"What?" Pan asked. "When?"

"Before."

*Before* referred to their old lives as treasure hunters. Before me and Pan were born and Mum and Dad settled down as boring college professors. Before we learned about their past. Before they came out of retirement to stop the People of the Snake from hiding the truth about the lost civilization.

We checked into a small hotel on the east side of the River Tiber, an area called Trastevere. The hotel wasn't great – the ceilings were blotched with damp, and the taps groaned when you turned them on, as if they might suddenly explode. I wanted to go out and explore, but Dad insisted that our enemies might have followed us here, so the less time we spent in the open the better. But Rome was right outside! In the end he agreed the three of us could go up to the hotel roof to see the city while Mum went to get us some food.

The hotel may have been shabby, but that view was incredible: a patchwork of terracotta-tiled roofs and church towers, grand marble domes, and even an Egyptian obelisk, although I've no idea what *that* was about. The sun was setting, causing the rooftops to glow pink and purple and dazzling gold, like the contents of a treasure chest had been spilled across the horizon.

I thought Dad might lecture us about the city's history, but instead he just sat staring across the skyline. He had that weird look on his face again – furrowed brow, sunken eyebrows, lost in thought.

"You all right, Dad?" I asked.

He looked at me, his eyes big and bulbous behind thick-lensed glasses. I expected him to smile – that's what parents do when you ask them if they're OK, even if they are very far from OK. But he didn't smile.

"I want you both to promise me something," he said.

"Okaaaay," Pan muttered. "Depends what."

"No, it doesn't," Dad replied. "This is non-negotiable."

The intensity of his glare was starting to scare me a little.

"What is it?" I asked.

He cleared his throat and looked back out across the city skyline. "If something happens to your mother and me," he said, "you have to promise not to carry on. You know where everything is. Find it and use it to return home. People there will look after you. You cannot carry on with this hunt. If we are gone, for whatever reason and in whatever way, then it is over. You walk away."

He looked back to us, his eyes now as fierce and glaring as a wolf's.

"Promise me," he insisted.

I glanced at Pan, who chewed her cheek nervously. We understood what he meant. My parents had hidden stashes of money, fake IDs and other documents, which we could use to get back to England, in several places around the world. But that meant turning our backs on everything we'd worked for, and letting the People of the Snake win.

"Dad, we—"

"This is not negotiable, Jake. For you, particularly."

"Why me?"

"Because you're more likely to act rashly. You cannot seek revenge, you cannot continue on against the People of the Snake. Swear to me, both of you."

"OK," Pan said.

I was stunned that she agreed so quickly. I wondered if she felt it wasn't going to happen anyway, so she might as well agree.

"Why are you asking this now?" I asked. "Is it because of Tibet?"

Dad winced and closed his eyes, as if the memory caused him physical pain. "While we searched for you, praying you were alive," he said, "I hated myself."

"It wouldn't have been your fault," I said.

"Of course it would. We are your parents. We led you into this. We even trained you for it. We would have been totally responsible. Now we're approaching the end of this hunt."

"So that's good, right?" Pan asked.

Dad looked back out to the rooftops as the sun nudged the pointed top of a church dome. It looked as if it had been pierced and was spilling pure gold.

"No," he replied. "Usually that's when things get worse. You have to make that promise or we can't continue at all."

He was staring at me now, waiting for an answer. The truth is I didn't know that I could promise that, not honestly. We'd come so far, we couldn't give up – no matter what. But I didn't like this conversation at all, and wanted it to end, so I nodded.

"OK," I said.

"Say it."

"OK, I promise."

"Good," Dad said. And just like that his eyes softened and a smile creased his stubbly cheeks. "Now, time for a history lesson."

Mum joined us on the roof a few minutes later with the best ever takeaway pasta and a crazy-tasty dessert called tiramisu. We ate it all with our fingers as she and Dad pointed out every famous site we could see, and lectured us on its history. For a moment we forgot about our mission and the reason we were here. I even forgot about Dad's strange mood and the promise we'd just made. For a couple of hours, we were just a family on holiday.

I remember that evening so clearly.

Because after that everything went to pieces.

# 5

The Capitoline is one of the biggest museum complexes in Rome, and the most popular. We planned to get there late, when it wasn't so busy and we'd have space to study the artefact. But when we arrived – an hour before the museum closed – the forecourt was still rammed with tour groups, and actors dressed as Roman soldiers posing for photos.

The museum looked like a royal palace. Sweeping marble steps designed by Michelangelo (the artist, not the Ninja Turtle) led to a huge square with a statue of a Roman emperor on a horse in its centre. Someone must have got a bulk deal on marble, because almost everything was made of the stuff: the high window arches, the ornate balustrade framing the roof and the tiny statues of naked gods perched on its top, peering down as if they might spit on us.

Mum pulled her backpack tighter over her shoulder. Ever since we left Kathmandu, she'd insisted on carrying the crystal device. She wouldn't even let me *look* at it again.

"Come on," she said, "let's go inside."

We mingled with one of the tour groups going into the museum, entering a courtyard filled with massive statue fragments: the staring head of an emperor, and a stone foot so huge the full sculpture must have been bigger than Godzilla. In the next room were statues from Roman myths, including a bronze she-wolf feeding the twin babies Romulus and Remus, the mythical founders of Rome, and a marble boy plucking a thorn from his foot. Pan told me that these artworks once decorated the villas of Rome's posh senators, but who looks at their garden and thinks, *What this needs is a statue of a naked boy with a thorn in his foot?*

Pan wanted to look at everything, but Mum reminded her that we were here for only one artefact. We found it in the fourth room, among glass cases displaying pottery and coins. In the smallest case, tucked away in a corner, sat the coral-covered remains of the crystal device.

Dad leaned in so close that his breath misted the glass.

I crouched to read the plaque, which repeated what we already knew:

UNKNOWN ROMAN OBJECT
RECOVERED FROM A SHIPWRECK, TURKEY
DATE UNKNOWN

"So what now?" Pan asked.

"We need to examine this properly," Mum said.

"We need to steal it," I added.

"Borrow it," Mum corrected.

"We're going to break into this museum later and take it from the case," I replied. "How's that not stealing?"

"Because we will return it."

"OK, so we'll steal it and then give it back."

"Stop saying *steal*, Jake. We are not thieves. Do you have a plan?"

Actually, I almost did. Even as Mum and I were squabbling, my eyes had been shooting around the room, spotting security weaknesses. I saw alarm sensors, windows that could be forced open, fire alarms, skylights... A plan began to form, a way to break in and swipe the artefact. We'd need climbing gear, and technology to take out alarms and bypass CCTV systems, but it might work. I was just about to tell my family the plan, when a voice spoke from behind us.

"The Atlas family. How nice to see you."

# 6

We whirled around, ready to fight.

Pan adopted a kung-fu position, Mum and Dad stepped in front of us as they always did, no matter how often we proved that we could handle ourselves, and I reached into my pockets, groping for any weapon I might use against whoever had tracked us to the museum.

I expected to see one of the People of the Snake's mercenaries. Instead, we were greeted by the broad, warm smile of a short woman with massive, round glasses and a huge pile of grey hair that looked as if an animal was nesting somewhere in there. She carried a bundle of books, which she dropped as she thrust her arms out for a hug. She greeted us in a thick Italian accent.

"John! Jane! *Bellissimo!* What a treat!"

For a moment none of us moved. Pan looked so tense I thought she might attack the woman. Finally, Mum burst out laughing and threw herself into the embrace.

"Elena? My God, is that you?" she said.

Dad laughed and hugged her too.

"How long has it been?" Elena asked. "Twenty years? Are these your children? *Che bello bambini!*"

She pinched my cheek with one hand, and went for Pan's with the other, but my sister stepped back sharply. The woman smelled of perfume and cigarettes.

"Children," Dad said, "this is Professor Elena de Mosto, one of the world's leading experts on Ancient Rome."

"For my sins," the professor added, which was one of those weird things adults said. "So what brings you to Rome?"

"A weekend break," Dad replied, a little too quickly. "We're introducing the children to the Eternal City."

"*Bellisimo!* The first of many visits, I hope."

She shot out a wrinkled hand, managing this time to pinch Pan's cheek. "*Buongiorno ragazza!* What interesting make-up you wear. Black is a much underused shade of lipstick. Now tell me, have you seen anything interesting so far?"

Pan did not look happy, but she sensed the chance to find out more about the coral-covered relic. She put on a good act, shrugging and looking vaguely around the room before waggling a hand at the artefact in the case.

"What about this thing?" she asked. "Looks a bit weird."

The professor glanced at the case, and then at Pan, and for a moment I spotted something other than delight in her face. It was hard to tell behind those thick lenses, but I swear her eyes narrowed just a fraction.

"How interesting," she said. "But let us get out of this chilly hall. Come to my office and I will tell you all about it."

My parents agreed, but as we followed the professor, Pan threw me a frown that meant *Does this seem fishy?* I fired one back: *Definitely.*

Elena opened a door with a security pass and led us up a stone staircase to a library that was almost as large as the hall downstairs. Leather-bound books were stacked so high that some could be reached only by using ladders that slid along the shelves. Golden shafts of sunlight beamed from high windows, illuminating swirls of dust.

"The Capitoline library," Elena announced.

I heard a little gasp, and realized it came from my sister. Whatever suspicions she had were forgotten the moment she saw that library. She stared with wide-eyed wonder around the shelves.

"It's incredible," she breathed. "Are these all history books?"

Elena clapped her frail hands louder than seemed possible, and gave a wheezy, chain-smoker's chuckle. "I see your daughter is a historian too, Jane. How about you, Jake? Do you also have a passion for the ancient world?"

I shrugged. "I liked *Gladiator*."

She stared at me, her eyes big and round behind her glasses.

"He's not as stupid as he seems," Pan muttered.

Elena didn't look convinced, but she clapped again. "Now, let us learn about that little relic that aroused your curiosity."

She led us to an office at the end of the library, where she rummaged amid a vast pile of books and papers that balanced on a desk. She yanked a book from the bottom, miraculously avoiding sending the others toppling, like a magician pulling a tablecloth from underneath crockery.

The book was a catalogue of the museum's treasures. Elena set her mobile phone down on her desk, turned on a side light and flicked through the book until she found what she was looking for.

"Ah, here we are," she declared. "Artefact 3246, unknown Roman instrument. As it says on the display, the relic was found on a shipwreck off the coast of Turkey."

"What was the ship carrying?" Mum asked.

"Ah, that is one of the curious details. Our relic seems to have been the *only* item on board that ship."

"The archaeologists couldn't find the rest of the cargo?" I asked.

"No, young *signore*, there was no other cargo. The archaeologists were quite certain that was the only item on board. It is curious, to say the least."

"Where was the ship found, exactly?" Dad asked.

"Another strange detail! The ship sank close to Odessa, in the Black Sea."

Mum and Dad spoke at the same time. "That's impossible."

Mum moved closer to Elena, double-checking the information in the catalogue. "We had assumed the wreck was off the *southern* coast of Turkey, in the Mediterranean," she said. "Roman ships often sailed those waters. The Black Sea, where the ship actually sank, is to the *north* of Turkey."

Pan could see I was struggling to keep up. "That was the far north of the Roman Empire, Jake," she said. "Roman ships hardly ever sailed there."

"Whose ship was it?" I asked.

"Aha!" Elena exclaimed. "That I *can* answer. We are quite certain that the vessel belonged to an individual named Marcus Turbo."

"*The* Marcus Turbo?" Mum asked.

The professor smiled and closed the catalogue. "The one and only."

"OK," I groaned, "you know I've no idea who that is."

"Turbo was a famous man in Ancient Rome,"

Dad explained. "A heroic soldier, and close friend of Emperor Hadrian. Many believed he would be chosen to succeed Hadrian as emperor."

"What happened to him?" Pan asked.

*"Uffa!"* Elena explained. "Another mystery." She blew on her fingers as if to clean away dust. "He disappeared."

"Disappeared?"

"Sometime around the year 130," Mum said, "Marcus Turbo vanished from Roman records. Perhaps he died in battle, or fell out of favour with the emperor. The rulers of Rome were notoriously fickle with their affections."

"Could he have drowned in the shipwreck?" Pan asked.

"It is unlikely he was on board," Elena replied. "It was a cargo ship, an uncomfortable vessel for a man of such status."

"So how do you know it was his ship?" I asked.

"Ah, that part is easy," Elena answered. "The ship carried his emblem on a brass plaque on its stern. I have a picture of it here..."

She rummaged around her desk again, and repeated the magic trick of removing a single book from the bottom without upsetting any of the others. She plonked it on top of the catalogue and flicked to a photograph from the archaeological report of the shipwreck. "Yes, here it is – a fairly distinctive symbol."

She moved the desk lamp closer so we could see the image. It was blurry, taken underwater, but clear enough to make out the engraved symbol. I was impressed with my family at that moment. None of us showed any reaction at all as we shuffled closer and stared at the emblem of this Ancient Roman superstar.

A snake eating its own tail.

# 7

The ouroboros.

I remembered with a chill the wise man's warning in Kathmandu that the symbol represented a cycle of destruction. It decorated the lost civilization's tombs, it was carved on the back of their crystal device and now here it was on an Ancient Roman shipwreck.

The professor looked at each of us in turn, her eyes narrowed behind her thick-lensed glasses. With a painted fingernail, she tapped the photograph in the archaeological report.

"Do you recognize this sign?" she asked.

Dad stepped back from the book and shrugged. "Of course we recognize it," he muttered. "As do you, Elena."

She chuckled; it turned into a hacking cough.

"The ouroboros," she said, finally. "A curious symbol, is it not? Somehow it was important to the Egyptians, and to Mesopotamian cultures. The Greeks, too, used it in their magical texts. But by Roman times it seemed to have meaning to only one person."

"Marcus Turbo," Pan said.

I noticed Mum touch her backpack and wondered if she was considering showing Elena the crystal device. If so, she decided against it, and her hand returned to the report on the table.

"So in the Roman world, the symbol only appears on this shipwreck?" she asked.

The professor eyed Mum curiously. A slight smile curled the corner of her mouth.

"There are other examples," she croaked, "but most are associated with Turbo. Some historians believe it to be the sign of a mysterious cult, a secret religious group to which Turbo possibly belonged. That is speculation. We do know that he adopted the symbol as his standard."

"His standard?" I asked.

"The symbol of his army legion," Pan explained. "The Roman army was divided into legions, each of around five thousand soldiers. They were competitive, tribal even. Like football teams, they each had a special sign they carried into battle."

*"Sei magnifica!"* Elena exclaimed. "What a clever girl! Except Marcus Turbo did not command a legion. He led the Praetorian Guard."

"The Praetorians were elite soldiers," Dad added, anticipating my question. "Like today's Special Forces.

Mainly they guarded the emperor, but they also undertook particularly dangerous missions."

"Perhaps Marcus Turbo simply liked the look of the ouroboros," Mum suggested. "So he adopted it as his standard."

Even as she said that, Mum didn't sound like she believed it. It wasn't just that Turbo had used the symbol; his ship was also carrying a mechanism a lot like the one we found in Tibet. But how were they linked?

Elena snapped the book shut and glanced at her mobile phone. "Now, perhaps you would like to tell me what this is really about," she said.

She looked at us each in turn, and her smile widened. "I am old, but I am not blind. You came here to view one of our most obscure relics. You wish to know about its owner, and occurrences of this mysterious symbol. I admit, I am intrigued. This artefact and the symbol clearly mean something to you, and I would dearly love to know more. Do you remember the old days, Jane, before competition for funding became so fierce among historians? We used to share our secrets."

Mum and Dad exchanged another battle of looks. Dad even took his glasses off so Mum could better see his disapproving frown. But Mum simply nodded in reply, as if this was something we'd all agreed. She opened her backpack and brought out the crystal device.

She held the artefact under the lamplight and turned it over, revealing the snake symbol, glinting and perfect, on its back.

*"Mamma mia!"* the professor exclaimed. "Where is this from?"

"It's a long story," Dad explained. "We're trying to work it out. Elena, it is very important that we do."

I noticed Elena's hand tremble slightly, so close to something so ancient and pristine. She looked again at her phone.

"You believe this to be the same item as in this museum?" she asked.

"Possibly," Mum replied. "Elena, this might sound strange, but we believe this device predates Ancient Rome by thousands of years."

"How many thousand? It cannot be Egyptian or Sumerian. It is certainly not from the Indus Valley. Perhaps from Turkey, from Göbekli Tepe? That is the oldest known settlement."

"No, Elena, long before all of those."

"But ... there was no civilization before those. There is no proof."

"We've seen proof," Pan said. "Tombs, coffins, wall paintings, all belonging to a civilization that was wiped out by a terrible catastrophe."

"*Urca!* This is science fiction!"

"That's what I thought at first," Mum admitted. "But I've seen enough to know this is real. Look..."

She took her holosphere from her backpack and

tapped in the code to start it up. Elena shuffled closer, staring at the images projecting from the screen of things we'd discovered: tomb paintings in Egypt, Aztec temples decorated with the ouroboros, the lost civilization's crystal coffins.

Mum spoke in a whisper, like she was praying. "Elena, all those other civilizations – Egyptian, Indus, Sumerian – were a legacy of this one."

"A legacy?"

"You know ancient mythology better than any of us," Mum continued. "In the Epic of Gilgamesh, the Sumerians claimed strangers from a far-off land came to them on a flood to create their civilization. In Egypt, they described Osiris adrift on flood-waters, while the Aztecs spoke similarly of their god, Quetzalcoatl, or Viracocha to the Incas. Even Noah, in the Bible. They all arrived on floodwaters to form new civilizations after natural disasters destroyed their homelands."

Elena flapped a wrinkled hand, as if to swat a fly. She glanced again at her phone and then back to Mum.

"Jane, flood myths were central to *all* ancient cultures," she said. "Farming people lived and died according to the rhythms of nature. That is why they wrote so often of floods and natural phenomena."

"That's what I was taught too, Elena," Dad agreed, "until I saw evidence suggesting a different origin for those stories. A single ancient civilization, which was destroyed by some catastrophe, possibly a great deluge. Its survivors founded Ancient Egypt, Sumeria, Ancient China and others. There's evidence to suggest that whatever wiped them out may come again, maybe even soon."

"Then present this evidence for scrutiny," Elena insisted.

"Most of it has been destroyed," Pan explained.

"Who would destroy such things?"

At last something I could answer, and I seized the chance. "There's an organization that wants to hide all this," I said. "They think whatever wiped the civilization out will happen again and if people find out there will be chaos. So they want to keep it secret. We're trying to find the evidence first, to warn the world."

Elena gave a long exhale, as if blowing out candles on a birthday cake. She sagged into a leather chair, snatching another quick look at her phone. An alarm went off in my head, a warning signal that I should already have noticed.

"This is a lot to take in," Elena muttered.

"We don't expect you to believe every word," Dad replied. "We're just asking for a few minutes of your time. Can you study this artefact? Tell us as much about it as you can."

"I am afraid not, John."

"Please, Elena. Five minutes, and then we'll—"

"We don't have five minutes," I interrupted. "We're already out of time, aren't we, Professor?"

Her eyes met mine, huge and staring behind the thick lenses. She smiled again, but there was no joy in it this time. It came with a sigh, and a sad nod that caused her beehive hairdo to sway.

"Ah, little Jake," she said. "Perhaps you are the smartest here, after all. There is something that now you must see. It is from the Italian police."

She picked up her phone and opened an email to show us an attached document. There were four photos – one of each of us – taken by CCTV cameras at the airport in Rome. Below was a warning, written in red:

> **The following individuals are wanted for antiquity theft. They are known to target museums and should be considered highly dangerous. If seen, contact the number below but do not approach the suspects.**

Pan cursed and shoved a pile of books from Elena's desk in a sudden rage. "You called this number?" she demanded.

Elena raised her palms in surrender. "I did, before I approached you."

"Then you invited us up here until the police arrived," Dad said.

"What would you have done, John, if you received such a message?" Elena asked. "I had not seen you for twenty years. There were always rumours that you and Jane were involved in antiquity dealing. I refused to believe it back then. You were such passionate historians! It was impossible! But here you are with an astonishing relic, and little information as to its provenance."

Pan swore even louder. She was about to toss more books from the desk, but I grabbed her arm and held her back.

"It's not her fault, Pan," I said. "That message is from the police."

"The people who are coming *control* the police," Pan snapped, shaking me off. She glared at Elena. "They've destroyed tombs and blown up temples. They'd think nothing of tearing down this whole museum to get hold of this."

Pan snatched the crystal mechanism from the table and thrust it at the professor. Elena took off her glasses and rubbed her eyes wearily.

*"Mamma mia,"* she muttered. "What a mess."

"Everything we've told you is true," I insisted. "Something bad is going to happen – something that might kill millions – unless we can warn people. We need to find more evidence."

Elena's knees clicked as she rose from her chair. She picked up the books that Pan had hurled to the ground.

"I have done my job," she said, "and informed the police. But I am an old woman. I cannot keep you here against your will. Certainly I have not told you about any secret doors in this library, hidden behind books on the Roman army."

"Thank you, Elena," Mum said.

The old professor gathered several books in her arms, and shuffled back to the library shelves. She stopped and turned. "There is another thing you should know. The ouroboros appears in one other, curious location."

"Where?" Pan asked.

"The Basilica Julia, in the Forum," Elena replied. "Most historians think it is ancient graffiti, and so did I, but perhaps there is more to it. Either you are on the verge of the greatest discovery in history, or you are crazy people. Either way, *buona fortuna*."

# 8

Finding the library's secret door wasn't hard – we were used to that kind of thing – but we were barely halfway down the stairs on the other side before we stopped in our tracks. A door at the bottom was open a fraction. Shouts from the other side rang up the narrow stairwell.

Pan peeked through.

"What do you see?" Dad asked.

"Trouble," she replied.

I edged closer to Pan to see for myself. In the museum hall, mercenaries in black military outfits ushered tourists towards a door, barking about security threats and safety measures. A few of the tourists protested, but most obliged, probably because the mercenaries had stun guns holstered at their belts. Few even complained when, before being guided out, they were asked to stare into a tablet computer screen.

"It's a facial recognition scanner," Pan muttered. "They're looking for us."

Despite her genius, my sister had a way of stating the obvious.

"I see eight mercenaries," Mum whispered.

"Can we fight that many?" Pan added.

"*We* cannot fight anyone," Dad hissed. "Your mother and I will do any fighting."

More shouts, now from the top of the stairs. The mercenaries had discovered the secret door from the library. They were coming...

"Stay behind us," Mum ordered. "Those stairs will lead to an exit. Once we're through, we run. Get in among the crowd, move with them. If we split up, meet back at the hotel."

"That didn't go so well last time," Pan noted.

"Stay clear of any trouble," Dad insisted. "Do not put yourselves in danger."

He reached and gripped my shoulder.

"Remember your promise," he said.

Again I felt that Dad sensed something we didn't, or feared something that none of us knew about, including himself. He'd been doing this for a long time, and his instincts were almost always right. This time, though, I felt it myself, too; something was wrong here. We'd spotted eight mercenaries, but we'd only been able to see in one direction along the hall. We had no idea what was really out there. I was about to say as much, but just then Mum barged through door and into the hall. Dad followed, and then Pan. All I could do was rush after them, praying I was wrong.

"Oh, God," Pan gasped.

We stood as still as the statues that lined the hall, staring in the other direction from the door we'd hoped to escape through. At least fifty goons dressed in combat suits and smart-goggles packed the hall, each with an electrolaser stun gun aimed at us.

"Go back!" Mum yelled.

But there was no way back. Shadows stretched down the stairs to the library. They were coming from that way too.

Behind us, mercenaries shoved the last of the tourists out of the hall and guarded the exit. Eight to one side, fifty to the other. The group by the door parted slightly to allow someone to walk through.

"You would not believe," the person said, "how much we have paid these mercenaries in overtime just to track down one family."

I recognized the voice, which sounded like a member of the Royal Family – deep, English and reeking of poshness.

"Oh, great," I groaned. "*Him.*"

Lord Osthwait was one of the leaders of the People of the Snake, and an all-round nitwit. He *looked* like royalty. His salt-and-pepper hair was immaculately parted, and his moustache belonged in the nineteenth century; it was bushy, and twirled slightly at the ends. He wore the same huge fur coat he'd had when he'd tried to catch me in Tibet. I've no idea what animal it was stripped from, but it must have been the *whole* animal; it was amazing that the weight of the thing didn't send him toppling over. Leaning on an ivory-topped cane, he stepped away from the mercenaries.

"At least it was money well spent," he added. "Now, perhaps we could avoid any pointless unpleasantries and you could simply hand over the key?"

I think all four of us were about to yell something nasty at him – although I suspected from the look on her face that Pan's would have been the nastiest – but the words caught in our throats. What had he said?

"Key?" I asked.

"The artefact you located in Tibet," he explained.

Something strange happened then: Mum laughed. An actual, proper laugh that surprised the mercenaries so much they all turned their weapons towards her.

"You don't know what it is, do you?" she said. "What we found in Tibet. You don't even know what it looks like."

"I know far more than you imagine," Osthwait declared. "I have not seen the artefact in question, but I certainly know its importance. I know, also, that by withholding it you are putting many, many lives at risk. Not least those of your children."

"They can look after themselves," Mum shot back.

"Of that I am also fully aware," Osthwait agreed.

"We do not need to be enemies. We are working towards the same goal."

"The same goal?" I scoffed. "You want to hide a catastrophe that may kill millions."

"No," he insisted, "that is not our goal. Not anymore. The device you have in your possession could stop that catastrophe from happening. But you must deliver it to me."

"Jane," Dad muttered, "maybe we should at least listen to—"

"If you want it, come and get it," Mum snapped, ignoring Dad. "But know that if you try, you'll also be paying these mercenaries' hospital bills."

Lord Osthwait sighed so heavily that his moustache rustled. "Very well," he said. The mercenaries parted again. One of them opened the door to the stairs, and Osthwait left, barking a final command to his goons.

"Take them!"

Both groups of mercenaries started roaring orders, and shuffling closer to us. I turned, and turned again, looking for any other way out.

"Jake," Mum called, "what's the plan?"

I breathed in, held my breath for a few seconds, and then let it go – a calming technique to help me think clearly. There was no way we could fight this many mercenaries, so we needed another escape plan. I remembered the market in Kathmandu, and how I had got away...

"The device," I called.

"What?" Pan cried.

"The crystal device. Turn one of the cogs."

"Jake," Mum snapped, "we need a plan, to—"

"This is my plan! Just do it."

Mum was about to protest again, but Dad cut her off. "Jane, we're out of ideas. It's worth a go."

Mum cursed, but yanked the device from her backpack. The mercenaries had obviously been told what to look for, because the moment they saw the artefact they yelled even louder for us to hand it over. They shuffled closer, now ten metres from us on either side.

"Now, Mum!" I called.

"Jake, this is—"

"Now!"

Mum's finger shook as she touched one of the mechanism's crystal cogs. She turned it several clicks.

Nothing happened.

"Great," Mum groaned.

She put the device back into the backpack and tossed it to me. "New plan. Your father and I fight while you two find a way out. Take that bag and get as far from here as possible."

This didn't sound good. We'd split up on missions before and it always led to trouble. We worked better together, whatever the danger.

"No, Mum," I protested, "we can—"

At that moment the hall jolted. Mercenaries cried out and stumbled into one another. Statues tumbled from plinths and smashed across the marble floor.

"Get down!" Dad yelled. "Cover your heads!"

A glass display case exploded. Now another shattered, and another, then one of the windows, showering the hall with glass. Mum yanked me to the floor as the hall shook even harder and more and more statues fell.

"What's going on?" Pan screamed.

"It's an earthquake," Mum called.

"It's not!" I cried. "It's the device!"

The mercenaries guarding the exit tried to pull the door open, but something had jammed it shut. One of them fired at it with a stun blast and they staggered back as sparks ricocheted. The others grabbed the door handles, but lurched back in shock.

Black smoke drifted through cracks around the door.

It was as if there was a fire outside, only this smoke moved unlike any I'd seen. Instead of just rising, it spread in different directions as it came thicker and faster from the edges of the door. It was like a living thing. Black tendrils slid down the door and along the ground as more floated upwards, circling around the ceiling.

"What is that stuff?" Pan gasped.

The hall shook harder. Lights fell from the ceiling

and shattered around us. A zigzag crack opened in the marble floor...

The mercenaries tumbled back as the smoke continued to flow into the hall. Suddenly, a cloud of it rushed at them like an animal, pouncing at the mercenaries and swallowing them completely. I heard no screams or shouts. All eight of them just vanished.

The smoke continued to gather, moving towards us.

"Get back!" Dad yelled. "Get away from it!"

Most of the mercenaries in the other direction had fled, but a few stood their ground, still aiming their stun guns at us. More cracks in the floor split even wider. Chunks of marble fell away and crashed down to whatever part of the museum was below.

I pulled my smart-goggles from my pocket and gave them a wheezed instruction. *"Satellite view."*

The lenses presented a fuzzy birds-eye view of the museum: the square at the front, and a smaller one at the back, with some sort of ornament in the centre. It was tricky to tell with the sweat in my eyes and lenses shaking, but it looked like a fountain. There was a window directly above it, one floor down from where we were.

I shoved the goggles into the backpack, unsure if I should tell my family my plan. Part of me felt safer here among the mercenaries, in the shaking room with the freakish smoke.

"We have to move!" Mum called. "The floor is about to collapse..."

"No, we have to go with it!" I yelled. "There's a window at the end of the hall below. We can jump into a fountain. But the only way down is *with* this floor. Unless you want to take a chance with whatever *that* is."

The smoke drifted even closer. The room shook even harder. The cracks across the floor spread even wider.

"OK, get ready!" Mum barked. "Roll when you hit the ground, and keep moving. If you hesitate, you die."

I think that was her idea of a pep talk.

A slab of the marble floor rocked up and down and then fell, taking us with it. We dropped twenty feet, screaming the whole way, and landed in rubble. Dad yanked me away, seconds before a slab of marble crashed down where I'd just been.

"Move!" Dad roared. "Get up and move!"

He pulled me up, and we all staggered towards the window. My vision was clouded with blood and dust and sweat.

Every display case had shattered or fallen. Ancient statues and vases lay in pieces amid rubble from the ceiling. Another chunk of marble landed ahead of us, along with a dozen mercenaries from upstairs. Maybe they were on bonus pay for catching us, because the moment they saw us, they raised their stun guns.

Mum was on them like a panther. She leaped and swiped, knocking a stun gun from a hand. Dad let go of me, and I fell to the floor as he joined Mum in the battle. He swung punches like a heavyweight boxer, knocking mercenaries over with single blows, while Mum leaped into high spinning kicks, then dropped low and swept away their legs.

"Jake, Pan, get out of here!" Dad hollered.

We yelled in protest, but we couldn't let the mercenaries get the device. The black smoke was coming after Mum and Dad now, sliding from the floor above and spreading out across what was left of the ceiling. It definitely wasn't normal smoke. It seemed alive, like it knew where we were.

"Come on, Jake!" Pan insisted.

As we scrambled over the rubble and past our parents and the mercenaries, I spotted something. Incredibly, the museum's crystal device was just lying there in my path. I didn't have time to consider how unlikely that was, or what that might mean – I just grabbed it and shoved it into my backpack with the other one, as Pan tugged me towards the end of the hall.

The window had shattered, and sunlight spilled through its arched frame. In the fountain below, a Roman god spurted water into a shaking, shallow pool.

"That's not deep enough to jump into," Pan cried.

I looked back. "Mum, Dad, hurry!"

They still had two mercenaries to deal with, but it felt like the whole building would cave in. Dad was about to punch one of the mercenaries, when he stopped and looked up. Above them, the smoke had gathered into something more like a storm cloud, shadowing my parents.

Dad turned and glared at us through cracked glasses.

"Do you remember your promise?" he roared.

"Dad, move!" I screamed.

"Tell me you remember," he insisted.

"I..."

I was about to yell again, but the words caught in my throat.

The black smoke dropped.

It engulfed Mum, Dad and the mercenaries. I tried to scream, but my mouth was suddenly bone-dry. It was all I could do to stand and stare as the smoke parted and drifted away from where my parents had been.

They were gone.

Completely gone.

Pan started to move back, but the smoke was coming for us now, and the museum was about to collapse.

I grabbed my sister's arm and yanked her into the sunlight.

# 9

Pan was right. The pool wasn't deep enough.

I burst to the surface, screaming from the pain where my side had hit the fountain's stone base. Pan was a few metres away on her hands and knees, gasping.

I helped her up and we leaned against each other for support. For a moment we stood, soaked and shaking, staring up at the Capitoline as its roof collapsed, showering tiles and statues down onto the square. A chunk of masonry the size of a wheelbarrow landed close by the fountain, spraying up water.

"It ... took them," Pan breathed.

No. Everything had been chaos and confusion. Maybe we just hadn't seen things clearly.

Pan grabbed my arm. "Jake, they were gone. The smoke, whatever that was... Mum and Dad weren't there anymore. What happened?"

"I – I don't know."

Pan was freaking out. She needed more than that.

"But they're still alive," I added.

"How do you know that?"

I didn't have an answer. I didn't even know if it was true. I waded to the edge of the fountain and climbed out. The museum had stopped shaking. From the other side of the building I heard police and ambulance sirens, and the combined wail of a hundred car alarms.

The black smoke had taken the mercenaries in the museum, but there would be other mercenaries. If they knew we'd escaped they'd come after us to get the crystal devices in my backpack.

"We have to get out of here," I mumbled.

I reached to help Pan from the fountain, and she took my hand. But her eyes remained on the window we'd jumped out of – where we'd last seen our parents. Her breath was ragged; she was almost hyperventilating. She was as confused and heartbroken as I was, but we needed to focus. My mind was in pieces, struggling to pull my thoughts together.

"Pan, we don't know what just happened," I said, as confidently as I could. "But maybe we can find out."

"So ... what should we do?"

"We have two devices, and a clue. Remember what Elena said about another ouroboros symbol somewhere here in Rome?"

"At the Forum, she said."

"Yeah, we'll find that. Hopefully we'll find some answers, and a way to get Mum and Dad back. If we stay around here, though, we'll get caught."

It was my best plan – my only plan – to try to make some sense out of this. But Pan shook her head.

"Jake, remember what we promised Dad? We said we wouldn't carry on if anything happened to them. We promised we'd quit the mission."

Of course I remembered – it was the last thing he said to us before … whatever just happened. But right then I didn't care. They were gone and we had to get them back. Nothing else mattered.

I wiped the wet hair from my eyes and pulled my backpack tighter around my back.

"The Forum, Pan. Where is it?"

# 10

"Oh, my God," I breathed.

I stared out across a field of devastation: crumbled buildings, fallen arches and crooked columns standing beside piles of rubble where others had totally collapsed. Some of the buildings still had walls, but most had been reduced to ruins.

"The whole city is destroyed," I gasped.

My sister looked at me. We hadn't had to run far from the museum, but she was struggling to catch her breath. "Jake, these are ancient ruins. This is the Roman Forum."

"Oh ... yeah. I mean, I knew that."

I'm no match for Pan's intelligence, but I did actually know that. We were still freaked out by what had happened in the museum, but our only hope of finding answers was to carry on with our mission. For that we needed Pan's brains, and few things focused her mind better than mocking my ignorance.

Word about the chaos at the museum must have spread, because the Forum was being shut down too. Police officers blew whistles, directing tourists towards exits at either end of the archaeological site. Since most people were leaving, no one at the entrance booth was looking out for anyone sneaking *in*, so it was easy to slip past the turnstile amid the crowds moving in the opposite direction. A few others remained among the ruins, stubbornly snapping a few last photos, but the police would spot us soon enough, and chuck us out. We had a few minutes, at best, to find Elena's clue.

We rushed down a zigzag path.

"What was this place, exactly?" I asked.

"The Forum was the heart of ancient Rome," Pan explained. "Roman senators decided new laws in some of these buildings, and others were temples. There were triumphal arches to celebrate military victories, and a road where the Roman army had parades."

The things she pointed at looked the same to me – a sprawl of rubble and ruin. It was hard to imagine the site as different buildings, let alone as the centre of the Roman Empire. But beyond one of the exits, past a grand marble arch, stood something I did recognize: a huge round building, half ruined. It looked like a giant cake with a chunk cut out.

"That's the stadium from *Gladiator*!" I exclaimed.

"Jake, that's the Colosseum."

"Yeah, from *Gladiator*."

"Well, yes. It's where Romans watched gladiator fights and sports events."

"They should rebuild it like in the movie."

I was winding her up on purpose. The more annoyed Pan got with me, the more she was like her usual self. We needed that right now.

"Shut up, Jake. We need to find the Basilica Julia. That's where Elena said archaeologists discovered the snake symbol. And before you ask, the Basilica was a law court and meeting place for the city's leaders."

Pan pulled her smart-goggles from her pocket and slid them on. *"Site map, Roman Forum."* The lenses flickered, showing her a plan of the site. *"Locate Basilica Julia."*

She yanked the goggles off and grabbed my arm. "This way!"

We weaved among more ruins until we reached what I can only describe as a *larger* ruin. Pan said this was once an important government building, but you could have told me it was a temple or a bathhouse – or anything – and I'd not have known the difference. All that was left of the building were a dozen column bases laid out in a long rectangle, blocked off from tourists.

"You keep watch," Pan said. "I'll look."

Before I could agree, she leaped over the railing and began to hunt among the ruins, scurrying and crouching, examining every stone. I turned, watching the police officers guide the last tourists from the site. One of them spotted us and waved us over. I grinned and waved back.

"Pan," I hissed. "We've got one minute..."

"Jake!" she called. "Over here."

I jumped the rail and joined her as she rubbed dirt from one of the column bases to examine a vague, worn shape. Something was carved there, about the size of a dinner plate. Two thousand years of weather and pollution had eroded it until it was almost unrecognizable – but not to us.

"The ouroboros," Pan said. "But why is it here?"

I hoped she was asking a question that she was also about to answer, but her face remained blank as she stared at the symbol.

I turned and watched the police officers march closer.

"It could mean nothing," Pan suggested. "Just graffiti, like Elena said. Or maybe it led to something inside the Basilica that's long gone."

"What if it wasn't something inside the Basilica?" I asked.

"Well, that's even less helpful."

"No, what if it led to something *outside* of the building?"

"You mean if it was pointing to something?"

I think that's what I meant. It was hard to focus with the police getting closer. They were shouting to us now, and coming from all directions. I tried to put them out of my mind and concentrate.

"Elena said this symbol may be the sign of a secret religious group," I said.

"Yeah, a mystery cult."

"What else do you know about cults?"

"Well, they met in hidden locations, usually underground..." Her face lit up with sudden realization. "The *Cloaca Maxima*!"

"Eh?"

"The *Cloaca Maxima*, Jake. The Ancient Roman sewer."

"The Romans had sewers?"

"Of course! They were expert engineers. They built sewers, viaducts, roads, underfloor heating, plumbing, flushing toilets—"

"OK, but what about this sewer? The maxy cloaky thing."

"The Cloaca Maxima. It means Great Drain. It runs right under the Forum and feeds into the River Tiber half a mile away."

"*Runs?* It's still there?"

"There's even a way in, close to here."

"Does it have an iron door?"

Ten metres away, a flight of stone steps covered by a tiled arch led down to a rusty iron door. The door didn't look like an important stop on a tour of Rome. I doubted many tourists even noticed it, but Pan looked like she'd just discovered a lost tomb.

Shrieking, she rushed down the steps.

"Jake! Do you think the symbol was guiding us here?"

I wasn't sure, but it seemed possible. And, anyway, we couldn't stay in the open any longer. One of the police officers blew a whistle, and I heard boots marching along the paths between the ruins. But by the time the officers reached the Basilica, we were gone.

# 11

"Oh, gross!"

I pressed an arm over my mouth, partly to muffle my voice, but mainly to stifle the reek of the ancient tunnel. A few stone steps led from the entrance to the Cloaca Maxima to a thick, oozing underground stream that seriously stank.

I slid on my smart-goggles and shone their torch around the ancient tunnel. The light glimmered off stalactites of filth that dangled from the sewer ceiling. The arched tunnel walls were slicked with grease and grime, as if a giant slug had slithered over them. A river of foul-smelling muck ran into the darkness. Actually, *river* isn't the word. Rivers flow. This was just a pool of sewage. My torch picked out fast-food wrappers and used nappies in its curdled brown surface.

"Pan, you didn't say this was *still* a sewer."

She spoke from behind her own arm-muffler. "It's

not, officially, but locals use it to dump stuff. Hotels empty cesspits in here, as well as rubbish and cooking fat, which is as gross as it is illegal. It all flows out into the River Tiber."

"Flows?"

"Stop being a baby, Jake. We're on a mission."

She was right. Actually, the grossness of this place was a welcome distraction from everything that had happened above ground. When faced with a river of sewage it's surprisingly easy to forget that your parents recently vanished in a cloud of smoke.

Pan stepped down into the slurry. The squelch was gross, but it was even worse to see how slowly she sank into the stuff. It was as thick as treacle.

"Come on," she said, now waist-deep in the stream. "If that symbol was leading us down here, there may be some sort of cult chamber hidden along the tunnel."

"Is it warm?"

"Eh?"

"The sewage."

"Just get in, will you! The People of the Snake may know about Elena's clue. They could be on their way, so we have to move fast."

I hitched my backpack strap tighter against my shoulder and slid one leg into the filth, feeling it thick and sticky against my thigh. It *was* warm, almost like stew. Pan led the way, squelching slowly through it.

"It's incredible, isn't it?" she whispered.

"Incredibly gross, you mean?" I groaned as I began wading after her.

"No, Jake. Without this sewer Rome wouldn't have existed. The River Tiber was always flooding. This sewer drained the land so the city could grow. It's one of the Romans' most important building projects, but hardly anyone knows it's here."

It was weird to be in an Ancient Roman structure that hadn't been destroyed, even though the grossness of the place didn't exactly make it a tourist hotspot. Here and there stone blocks had fallen from the walls, and creatures scurried in the gaps. Squeaks echoed down the tunnel.

"Rats," I breathed.

We edged closer together as Pan remembered something else she'd read about this tunnel. "Millions of rats live down here," she said. "It's a perfect home, with so many restaurants dumping old food."

Tiny eyes gleamed in my torchlight. One of the rodents gave a shrill warning. My hand tightened on Pan's arm.

"Jake, we've faced giant mutant snakes, drone attacks and deadly traps in ancient tombs... Are you really scared of a few rats?"

I had a feeling there were more than a *few* rats down here. I gave my goggles a whispered instruction. *"Thermal."*

The torch cut out, and the lenses switched to a thermal imaging camera that showed heat signatures of living things as glowing orange blobs.

"Oh, God," I groaned.

Everywhere I looked – up and down the tunnel, above us and even in the filth below – orange blobs glowed. Thousands and thousands of rats.

"Come on," Pan said.

We kept moving. Our torchlight swept the walls, and glimmered off sewage that seemed to grow thicker with every step. A clue to a secret chamber would be impossible to spot among all this filth. The longer we were down here, the more our thoughts drifted back to what had happened in the museum.

"Jake," Pan asked, "that smoke wasn't just smoke, was it?"

"I don't think so."

"What *do* you think?"

What could I say? I had an idea, but it sounded totally crazy...

"I think it was the crystal device. Turning its cogs unleashed ... *something*. It happened at the market in Kathmandu too."

"I thought you made that up."

"Well, it *sounds* made up."

"Whatever it was, do you think that's what destroyed the lost civilization? But how is it related to Marcus Turbo, and the snake symbol?"

A grunt was as much of an answer as I could offer. I shone my torch at a metal fitting in the sewer wall like an iron coat hook.

"Hey, what's this?"

"Looks like a bracket for a torch or lamp. There's another one over here."

The second one was five metres further along the arched wall, at head height. I turned, shining my light back along the tunnel, but these were the only brackets we'd passed.

"They must have been used to light the tunnel," Pan added.

"But why?"

"To see, Jake."

"No, I mean why here? Why was *this* the only place where the Romans needed to see something?"

I sloshed to the wall between the brackets and scraped filth from the stone. I hoped to see another snake symbol, but the surface looked the same as everywhere else. I waded a few metres along the wall and cleared away more of the muck. The wall there was set back slightly, as if it had sunk a few centimetres into itself. There were scratches in the stone, grooves where something had scraped against it.

Pan's eyes sparkled in the light from my torch.

"Secret door?" she suggested.

I took hold of one of the light brackets and tugged. The iron hook shifted in its groove, and a rumble like distant thunder echoed from behind. A section of wall slid forward, then scraped to the side.

*"Secret door,"* we said at the same time.

That was all we managed to say before a gust of

rancid air rushed out of the darkness. I staggered back, swatting at it.

"Gross!"

"It's been sealed for two thousand years, Jake. Of course it stinks."

Pan edged closer to the opening, using her torch to scan a small round chamber beyond. A year ago we'd have rushed in, but training and experience had taught us caution. For several minutes we remained in the tunnel, examining the chamber with our goggles' infrared vision, night vision and thermal imaging. There may have been a lot of rats in there, but nothing else was alive.

Together, we entered.

# 12

Slowly, side by side, we entered the chamber. I guided my torch around a domed ceiling that was low enough to touch, not that you'd want to. Lines of foul ooze ran down the walls, obscuring two-thousand-year-old frescoes that decorated the entire chamber.

"Jake, this is incredible..."

The sewage here was shallower – ankle deep. Sloshing through it, we moved around the room studying the paintings. There were three scenes, all showing figures in red and silver in different locations. I'd seen enough movies to recognize them as Roman soldiers. In one painting they were marching through a desert. In another they were on a ship, sailing over choppy seas. The third showed them fighting an enemy outside a fort. In each scene, something weird floated above the soldiers – a white disc, like a UFO.

"These are Roman legionaries?" I asked.

"Not quite," Pan replied. "Legionaries were foot soldiers. These are Praetorian Guards."

"How do you know?"

"Their shields are oval rather than rectangular. And legionaries wore sandals with leather straps, called *caligae*. But senior soldiers had leather boots, *calcei*, like the ones in these scenes."

"Huh," I muttered, trying not to sound impressed. "Wait, didn't Elena say that Marcus Turbo led the Praetorians?"

Pan nodded slowly. Usually we'd have been buzzing from a discovery like this, but not while our parents were missing. We needed a clue to what happened to them.

My sister shone her torch at one of the discs hovering over the soldiers. "I think that represents the crystal device. And look..." She turned her light to the painting of the ship, with the same hovering disc. "The museum's device was discovered in a shipwreck, remember."

"You think this is meant to be that ship?"

"Maybe... Look at these other two scenes. In each, the Praetorians are with one of the devices; three in total."

"Plus the one from Tibet makes four."

"Yeah, and it looks like they were taking them somewhere. But where, and why, and why did the Praetorians even have them?"

I didn't answer, and not only because I had no answer. My torch had found something else at the side of the dank chamber. Slumped against the wall, its head and chest above the sewage, was a human skeleton.

"Um, Pan?" I whispered.

She'd seen it too. She crouched closer to examine the skull with her torch. It stared back at us with hollow eyes, while its jaw hung open in a silent scream. The skeleton would have collapsed had it not been for a golden breastplate – armour – and a ragged white robe under it, which held the whole thing together.

I slid back, feeling a chill that had nothing to do with the cold underground air. We'd seen a fair few skeletons over the past year, but there was something particularly creepy about this one. Whoever it was had died alone down here in the dark...

Pan seemed fascinated by the skeleton's armour. She was leaning a little closer to examine the breastplate when something moved inside the skull. We staggered back, our screams turning into relieved laughter as a fat black rat squeezed through one of the skull's eye sockets and belly-flopped into the sewage.

"OK," Pan gasped, "so who is this guy? What is this place? And how does any of this help us find out what happened to Mum and Dad?"

A dull ache pounded the back of my head. We had

so many questions, but no answers. Was any of this leading anywhere, or was it all just one big riddle?

"Jake," Pan said, sensing my frustration, "maybe we should get out of here. Remember our promise to Dad?"

"No," I grumbled, "we need to keep looking. There *must* be a clue here."

"But, Jake..."

"Pan, we're not giving up."

She sighed, but could tell I wouldn't budge. I didn't care what I'd promised to our parents; there was no way we would walk away while there was a chance we could still save them.

Pan waded further along the wall, studying the mural that showed the soldiers marching through a desert surrounded by rust-coloured mountains. "There's Latin writing on this one," she muttered. "It says *Volubilis*."

"What does that mean?"

Pan knew the answer, but her voice suggested it still didn't make a lot of sense. "It's a place, a Roman city in Morocco. Why would they have taken one of the crystal devices there? It's almost like they were hiding them, but from who?"

I stared at the mural of the Praetorians guarding the fort. The soldiers stood on top of the fort wall, jabbing spears at an enemy who was hidden under the sewer grime. With my fingers, I scraped away the dirt to reveal the rest of the scene.

The chill inside me sharpened into a freeze, turning my insides to ice.

"Not who," I replied. "What."

In the scene, the Romans were fighting a cloud of smoke. *Black smoke.*

I was about to examine one of the other scenes when I noticed that the sewage we'd been wading through was gone. I shone my torch around the chamber floor, gobsmacked to see a bright and clean mosaic. It was a spotless white circle decorated with a familiar symbol – the ouroboros.

"What happened to the floor?" Pan asked.

It wasn't just the floor. The murals were now vivid and vibrant in my torchlight, as if they'd been painted last week. The skeleton was gone too.

"Um, that's seriously weird," Pan said.

A knot tied in my stomach, a feeling I only got when something very bad was about to happen...

"OK," I hissed, "let's get out of here."

From behind me came a sound. A sniff.

Pan heard it too.

"Jake..." she breathed.

"Pan... Sixteen."

That sounds like an odd reply, but it wasn't to Pan. Our parents had refused to teach us fighting skills, insisting we'd never need them. Since we did actually fight bad guys on every mission, Pan and I had invented moves of our own. Each one had a number we could call to coordinate our attack.

Another sniff. Louder, closer.

"*Sixteen*, Pan."

"I... Sixteen."

That was the signal. As soon as she repeated the number, we each counted to three in our head. This is what should have happened next: on three, we'd both drop to the ground and thrust backwards, so we'd crash into our enemy's legs and knock the person over.

But that didn't happen.

We fell to the mosaic and launched back, but the legs we hit were as strong as tree trunks and didn't budge. A hand grabbed the back of my neck. I swatted at it, but the grip grew tighter, lifting me from the ground. My smart-goggles fell off, and the torch cut out, plunging the chamber into darkness.

Pan turned and lashed out, but another arm knocked her back down.

The hand squeezed harder at my neck, strangling me. I grabbed one of its fingers and pulled until I heard a snap. At last, the person let go, and I fell to the ground beside my sister. Gasping, I scrabbled forward until I felt my goggles, shoved them on and wheezed a desperate command.

*"Super lumen..."*

A torch beam bright enough to light a football stadium shone at our attacker. I'd hoped to dazzle the person, but I hadn't expected it to work so *well*...

It was as if I'd thrown acid in the man's face. He

screamed and staggered back, shielding his eyes. I scrambled up, trying to gather strength to fight, but there was no need. Our attacker slumped back against the chamber wall. Even with my torch turned away, I could see the guy wore the same outfit that the skeleton had: a bronze breastplate over a white tunic. But this one was spotless.

The man's face was flat, like a boxer's, and his lips were dry and cracked, although I didn't notice at first because I was staring at his eyes. Or *eye* – one of them was missing. Its socket was shrivelled and dark, like a prune. The other eye blinked, struggling to recover from the torch glare. His mouth cracked open – I know people say that a lot, but I really did hear a crack as his lips peeled apart – and his words came out in a rasp.

*"Quis custodiet ipsos custodes?"*

I helped Pan up, relieved to see she was OK. We stood together, ready to fight.

"Is he speaking Italian?" I asked.

She shook her head. "Latin. It means, 'Who will guard the guards themselves?'"

That may have been what he said, but it didn't mean anything. "If he lives here, we should tell someone," I muttered, "or get him some food and blankets and—"

"Jake, I don't think he's homeless."

"Well, maybe he's one of those actors in fake Roman army kit."

"No, I don't think that kit is fake. Look at his sandals. *Calcei*, not *caligae*."

I remembered – a sign of a Praetorian Guard. "OK, so where did he get them?"

"I ... I think they're his."

I stared at Pan, and then at the soldier, and then back at Pan, struggling to make sense of what she'd said. "You mean... What do you mean?"

"I mean, this is an actual Praetorian Guard."

"What do you *mean*?"

"Jake, I mean—"

"I know what you mean, but that's crazy! Ancient Rome, Pan. That was ten thousand years ago."

"Two thousand. Although it depends on what period of Roman history you—"

"What *are* you saying, then? That this guy has somehow lived down here since then?"

"I'm – I'm not sure... Oh, God, he's getting up!"

The man rose from the chamber floor, his one good eye glaring at us in a way that suggested he planned to tear our limbs from our bodies, just for starters. I tried to think of one of our rehearsed fighting moves, but another plan popped into my head instead. If this guy was a real Praetorian, and he knew about this chamber, then maybe I was carrying a weapon of my own...

I swung my bag from my shoulder, pulled out one of the crystal devices and shoved the artefact at his face.

"Back off or I'll turn the cogs!" I yelled.

Pan didn't need to translate. The moment the guy saw the thing, his one eye bulged and veins throbbed in his neck as he roared at us like a deranged gorilla, spraying spit. He reached to snatch the relic from my hand, but I held a finger over its clockwork mechanism.

"Back off, I said!"

His hand rose from his sword and he edged back, watching me carefully as he growled something in Latin.

"He said, 'Don't do it'," Pan translated.

"Tell him that we're going to ask some questions," I replied, "and he'd better answer or I'll use this thing."

"Jake," Pan hissed, "maybe we—"

"Pan, I have no idea what's going on here, but this guy can give us some answers."

My sister muttered something disapproving, but finally agreed, translating everything I said and then the soldier's replies. His Latin wasn't quite the same as the Latin she knew, and the guy was pretty confused - not just by what Pan said, but by *us*. He reached out to touch the smart-goggles hanging from my pocket, but snapped his hand back, scared of the technology.

"What tribe are you?" he snarled.

"Tribe?" Pan asked.

"Has Rome fallen to your people?"

"I... No. We're British."

"Britannia?"

"Yes! Britannia. But we're... " Pan looked to me, wiping sewer muck from her eyes. "How do I tell him this?"

I shrugged. "Don't. It'll freak him out."

She turned back to the soldier. "How long have you been here?"

"Many years. I do not know how many. It is my duty to defend this sanctuary. You are infants. I will not kill you if you give me that key and speak nothing of this place."

"Jake," Pan hissed, "he called it a key, just like Lord Osthwait at the museum..."

I'd noticed, and it had confused me even more. "Why did you call this a key?" I demanded. "What is this thing?"

Pan translated my questions, but the soldier shook his head and asked us another in reply.

"Where did you find it?"

"In a mountain," Pan explained. "It was hidden there by the people that made it. Do you know about them?"

"I know that you children do not understand the power of what you hold. I cannot tell you any more. I am sworn to protect those keys."

"How many others are there?" Pan asked. "You found them somewhere, and brought them back to Rome."

"Never to Rome," he insisted. "We protect Rome. Those keys could destroy the Empire."

Pan turned back to the murals, guiding her torch around their details. Each showed the Praetorian guards in a different place, marching with one of the crystal devices.

"I think they separated the devices, Jake. They took them to different places, far apart from each other."

Still holding the device, I edged over to one of the murals and pointed to the black smoke in the scene. "What is *this*?" I demanded. "This took our parents."

"You have seen it?" the man grunted. "Yet you are alive..."

"Our parents. Are they ... alive?" Pan asked.

His eyes remained fixed on the device in my hand – the *key* – as he nodded slowly. "They are. If you can call it living. The smoke. As long as it has power in our world, it can hold them in its own realm."

"How do we get them back?" Pan pressed.

"There is only one way. You must defeat the smoke."

"How?" I demanded. "Tell us, what is the black smoke?"

"It is coming back. Soon..."

More riddles! I was about to threaten him again with the device, but right then a thin, dark wisp emerged from the screwed-up hole of the soldier's missing eye.

"Jake..." Pan hissed. "Do you see that?"

We edged back, watching in horror as the wisp grew thicker, curling like a tentacle. Black smoke.

The soldier stood totally still, staring at us with his other eye, his mouth hanging open and his arms flopping at his sides. The smoke from his eye spread, drifting towards us. Now it came from his mouth too, and then his ears. It looked like a gigantic spider trying to break free of his head.

A voice came from the soldier's mouth, although I don't think it was him speaking. It was a whisper, deep and echoey. One word.

*"Run."*

Then the soldier vanished.

I was breathing so hard that my chest ached. I looked down, saw that my feet were once again deep in sewage. Pan's torch shone on walls that were slick with slime. It was all gross and stinky, just as it had been a few minutes earlier.

And there was a noise.

A splash. Out in the tunnel something moved through the sewage.

"Jake," Pan hissed. "What just happened?"

I had no idea, but something was happening now. Someone was coming.

"We really need to get out of here," I whispered.

I shoved the key with the other one in my backpack and wc waded tu the chamber entrance. More splashes echoed from the direction we'd come from.

It sounded like several people moving along the sewer.

We shrank back as a torch beam shone past the chamber entrance and along the tunnel. Another ribbon of light rose around the sewer ceiling, then others, as mercenaries scanned the sewer. This wasn't good; we couldn't stay in the chamber, but if we waded back into the tunnel we'd be seen.

The answer was obvious to us both.

"Don't say it, Jake," Pan whispered. "Don't you dare say it."

"We have to crawl, Pan."

"Great, you said it."

I wasn't keen on the idea either, but it was the only way to avoid being spotted. The torch beams shone brighter as the mercenaries stalked closer along the tunnel. They were searching for us fleeing *through* the sewage; maybe they'd not think to look down among the sewage.

Pan swore at me as if this was all my fault, and then she sank into the sewage. There was a gross sucking sound as she began to crawl through the filth, her head just high enough above it to breathe.

I cursed under my breath, then got down on my hands and knees in the muck too. I clamped my mouth shut and closed my eyes, telling myself I was in a pool of chocolate mousse. It *felt* like mousse, thick and sticky. As I crawled from the chamber and into the tunnel, turning away from the mercenaries, my hands squelched against unseen horrors on the sewer floor.

Filth flicked up at my mouth. It took everything I had not to scream. Instead I spat, sealed my mouth again and kept going. The mercenaries' whispered commands echoed along the arched darkness as their torch beams shone over our heads. This was working so far, but we were moving too slowly. They were going to catch us up.

I heard Pan gasp and grunt, and guessed she was also struggling to stay silent as sewage sloshed up at her face.

Looking back, I saw the torchlights disappear into the secret chamber. Finally I rose from the sewage and whispered to Pan that it was safe to stand.

Just then a rat squeaked at me from a ledge. Another dropped from the sewer ceiling, hitting my head and splashing into the sewage. Suddenly dozens of them were scurrying past, as if *they* were being chased too.

Adrenaline spiked inside me, as I sensed something wrong – something other than the thugs hunting us in the dark. Behind us, the sewage seemed to be moving, writhing. It was the rats – there were thousands of them, swimming, and scurrying along the walls.

They were running from something.

"Jake..." Pan hissed.

"Just keep moving!"

I didn't know what else to say; our parents hadn't trained us to survive a rat stampede. One of them landed on my back and dug its claws into my shoulder. I shook it off, as more of them fell on Pan. She thrashed her arms and tried to swat them away.

"They're attacking us," she gasped.

No, they weren't after *us.* They were fleeing from something; we were just in the way. Several fell on me at the same time and my shriek rang along the tunnel. I shot a look back, but still couldn't see any torchlights. It didn't make sense. Would *all* the mercenaries have gone into the cult chamber? Surely some would stay in the tunnel to keep watch? Maybe they'd switched to night vision. Or maybe...

Or maybe they weren't there any more.

An alarm was going off inside me, a panic that had nothing to do with rats or mercenaries. As rodents writhed all over my body, I just managed to pull my smart-goggles from my pocket and gave them a whispered instruction.

*"Torch."*

A beam of light shone along the sewer, illuminating thousands of frantic, scrambling rats. I raised the torch, directing the shaky beam further down the tunnel.

"Oh, God..."

I stared at darkness. Not the darkness of the tunnel, but a black cloud that was moving *along* the tunnel, swallowing my torchlight as it drifted closer.

"Pan!" I screamed. "Run!"

But how can you run in knee-deep sewage? It felt as if I was moving through cement. Rats scrabbled over my back, digging in claws. Somehow they knew that the black smoke was dangerous. One of them scratched my cheek, another bit my thigh. Pan cried out, swatting and slapping.

"Pan!"

I kept calling, not because I could help her; just so she knew I was there. The rats were all over me. There wasn't a single part of me that wasn't covered with the creatures. The weight of them was like carrying another person on my back. I tried to keep moving, but slumped under the sewage, forced down by the weight of rodents. I fought back to the surface and gasped a lungful of rancid air.

Pan was on her knees in the sewage, buried under rats.

I managed to snatch a look back with my torch. The black smoke rolled closer, a moving wall, filling the tunnel, swallowing rats. Another rodent scratched my face and I sank again into the river of muck.

"Pan..." I groaned.

There was no escape. The smoke was going to catch us. It was all I could do to watch. Was I going to die?

"Jake!" Pan screamed. "Jake, we have to move!"

I couldn't. I was beaten.

The smoke was now a metre away. I could have reached out and touched it if I could move my arms.

"Jake, fight it! Whatever happens, survive!"

I heard her, but I had no idea what was about to happen, and that terrified me to the point that I couldn't even reply.

I closed my eyes and it took me.

# 13

Do you remember your dreams?

Dreams aren't things that have happened; they're not real memories. Usually I forget them a few minutes after waking. But this dream, if that's what it was, was different.

I remember it all.

I remember the face.

Not a human face, and not animal. Its features appeared and disappeared into an ash-grey cloud, swirling and reforming. The eyes were fierce and glaring, like those of a cornered tiger. Its mouth opened but no sound came out. It was strange to see something so aggressive but so silent, so vague and so sharp. It wasn't a trick of the mind, or a shape in smoke, the way people see Jesus on slices of toast. As the smoke rolled closer, it grew darker, the colour of midnight. The face appeared again, this time even more savage.

I thought it was glaring at *me*. But as I looked down from a hilltop, I realized it was vast – like a weather system – covering a valley and a city of white square houses, spiral ziggurats, and a pyramid that appeared black in the shadow of the smoke.

Fire rose from some of the houses. Others had collapsed, as if destroyed by an earthquake. The valley was shaking. Rocks tumbled down the hillsides, demolishing more of the buildings. Above the chaos, the smoke merged into a single, dense cloud. That was when I saw the face.

And then, nothing.

Darkness, wind, then shouts from a distance.

"Jake? Jake, I can't see!"

The black cloud swirled around me, slower now, and the visions faded. Hot wind lashed my eyes, and tiny, sharp stings, like needles, prickled my cheeks. It was sand, although I didn't know that then. I only knew three things: the black smoke had taken me, I was still alive, and I was no longer in a tunnel under Rome.

"Jake!"

I called back weakly, my throat parched in the wind, and swatted my arms to clear the last wisps of smoke. The world turned from black to dusty brown – a hillside covered in rock and scrub. I was *definitely* not in the tunnel under Rome.

Pan lay close by on the ground, her arms covering her face, screaming my name. I tried to lift her, but the moment I touched her she began to struggle, kicking her legs in wild panic.

"Pan! It's me. You're OK!"

She unpeeled her arms from her head and looked up through a mess of sewage-slicked hair. Her eyes struggled to focus and her lower lip trembled, as if part of her remained trapped in whatever nightmare she'd been experiencing.

I helped her stand and we leaned against each other, both of us breathing like we'd sprinted a hundred metres. I wiped sewage from my eyes and struggled to make sense of my new surroundings. We were high on a pass, gazing across a sea of grey-brown hills. In a valley below, a farmer herded goats, their bells tinkling lazily around their necks. A twist of smoke rose from a farmhouse chimney. Dimly, I remembered that the Cloaca Maxima fed into the River Tiber. Had we been washed downstream to somewhere outside Rome? At least I still had my backpack with the keys, even though it was soaked with sewage.

"Pan," I wheezed. "Where the hell are we?"

She pulled her smart-goggles from her pocket. They trembled in her hand as she slid them on. *"Situation report,"* she rasped.

Light flashed against her eyes as the lenses showed her GPS coordinates, satellite map views and topographical charts. Whatever she saw caused her ragged breath to suddenly stop, and then start again even faster.

"What the...?"

"Pan?" I asked. "What part of Rome are we in?"

"We're not in Rome," she replied. "Jake, we're not even in Italy."

*"What?"*

She pulled the goggles off and looked at them as if they were some alien object; baffled, surprised and scared all at the same time.

"According to these," she said, "we're in the Atlas Mountains."

She stared at me.

"In Morocco," she added.

# 14

It's not every day that you lose your parents to a smoke monster, travel two thousand years through time and teleport to a different continent.

We'd grown used to weird things, but the last few hours had gone way beyond weird. For about an hour neither of us could even talk about it. We stumbled along a dirt track until we hit a road that skirted the hill. At a stream, we washed sewage from our hair and faces, but our clothes were still soaked and stinky, and our shoes squelched with each step along the baking asphalt. It was early evening, but the sun was still savage. Like a playground bully, it hid behind small clouds, then popped out again to roast the backs of our necks.

According to our goggles, the nearest town, Fez, was four hours away on foot. We had no plan for when we got there, no money and no passports. All we had were our goggles and my backpack with the keys. We needed shade, water and rest. Maybe then – somehow – some of this madness might make sense.

We walked for an hour, sticking to patches of shadow thrown by the hills. Our clothes grew stiff as the sewage dried, and our cheeks became encrusted with salt from sweat. Wind whipped at our faces, and tiny dust tornados swirled up from the road. It was strange to feel so hot in such strong wind. It was as if someone was blasting us with a giant hairdryer. I couldn't even suck up enough spit to lick my lips.

We waved to a few passing cars and swore at them when they didn't stop. I didn't blame them, though; we must have looked pretty gross.

"So are we going to talk about it?" I asked, finally.

Pan mumbled, "Eh?"

She was stalling and I understood why. It was too freaky. Where did we start?

"What happened?" I pressed.

"Why do you think I know?" she snapped.

I didn't react. She was as confused as me, and as scared. But we needed to work together, not fight.

"I'm sorry," she muttered, as we carried on walking. "It's just... It's so weird. Let's go back and work our way forward. The black smoke, whatever it was, somehow took Mum and Dad. It took us, too, but it didn't kill us. It sent us here. So we have to hope it didn't kill Mum and Dad either."

"The Praetorian Guard said they were alive," I added.

She stared into the heat haze that shimmered across the road. "*That* was pretty weird."

"*Weird?* The way Dad snores is weird. Travelling back in time to meet an Ancient Roman soldier is something else."

"Do you think the smoke made it happen?"

I wasn't sure. Everything was confused. I was trying to think of the right questions, something that might help work this out.

"What was that smoke?" I asked.

"It's... It's something very powerful."

I glanced at Pan, sensing that she knew, or suspected, something about the smoke that she wasn't telling me. Maybe she noticed, because she quickly kept talking.

"The keys seem important to controlling it," she continued. "According to the chamber murals, the Praetorians found three of them somewhere, and then took them as far apart as possible. They tried to take one beyond the Red Sea, but the ship carrying it sank."

I swung my backpack from my shoulder and took out the key we'd stolen from the museum. "That was this key," I said. I slid it back in the bag and brought out the other one. "And this is the one the survivors of the lost civilization hid in Tibet."

"So there are two others," Pan said. "Is one of them

here, in Morocco? Is that why the smoke sent us here? But why, if it wants to *stop* us from finding them?"

"Wait, back up. *How* did we get here, Pan?"

I expected her to snap at me again for asking something she couldn't answer. Instead she burst out laughing, so loudly that pigeons flapped up from the side of the road.

"In Rome, the smoke sent us back through time, right?" she asked.

"I ... think so."

"Well, whatever it is, it also has the power to send us to different places."

Now I couldn't help laughing too. "Pan, that's crazy. Nothing has that power."

"Maybe not. I dunno."

We walked for a moment in silence, unsure what else to say. Did I believe any of this? I'd seen it with my own eyes. I'd spoken to an Ancient Roman soldier. I was in Morocco when I should have been in Rome. But, really, something else was on my mind...

"After the smoke took us," I asked, "did you see anything?"

"No, just darkness. What do you mean?"

What *did* I mean? Maybe the face had been a dream. For now we needed to focus on what we *did* know. "The Praetorian Guard said the only way to get Mum and Dad back was to defeat the smoke. These keys seem to be important to that, somehow, so we need to find them all."

"Maybe it's bigger than that, Jake. This smoke, whatever it is, I think it's what destroyed the lost civilization. That Roman soldier said it was coming back. So maybe this isn't just about saving Mum and Dad. Maybe it's..."

She sighed, unable to finish the sentence. We could handle saving our parents. That felt achievable – familiar, even. But stopping an unknown force from destroying the world? That was just nuts.

We both cracked up again.

"Save the world?" I said. "Some days I can barely tie my own shoelaces."

A bus honked its horn, warning us to move out of the way. We waved, and squealed with delight when it stopped. We were two filthy Western children alone in the middle of nowhere. The driver stared at us as if Bigfoot had appeared at the side of the road.

"Fez," I gasped to the driver. "Parents in Fez. Please take us?"

He signalled for us to climb on, and locals shifted up in their seats so we could squeeze in. Someone gave us water, and someone else offered us flatbread and a tasty aubergine dip, which we devoured between thank yous. We slept for a bit, and then I stared out of the window watching the sun sink below the hills, scattering the slopes with red and orange, as if the tips of the olive trees had been set on fire. I was about to fall asleep when Pan shook my shoulder.

"Jake, wake up!"

I rubbed my eyes and slid to where she was looking out of the window. The bus had stopped, and the driver was staring into the engine as black smoke gushed from one of the cylinders. We seemed to have broken down in the middle of nowhere. I rubbed mist from the glass to see road signs, names in Arabic and French. One sign pointed down a scruffy road, to what looked like a demolition site. Whatever it was, it had got Pan pretty excited.

"That's Volubilis," she breathed.

"It's what?"

"That's the archeological site of Volubilis, a Roman city at the very edge of the empire. Jake, it was on one of the murals in the cult chamber, remember? The Praetorians took a key here. We've broken down exactly where we need to search. Is that a coincidence?"

I shifted to see through the bus windscreen as the driver waved away the dark smoke from the clapped-out engine. I had no idea if it was a coincidence or not. We almost never "got lucky" on a treasure hunt, but maybe we had this time.

If so, we had to use that luck.

# 15

"Where Mum? Where Dad?"

A suspicious security guard eyed us from his ticket booth, a crooked wooden hut at the entrance to the ancient city of Volubilis. He used a fly swatter as a fan, but the armpits of his shirt were ringed with sweat.

"Don't be so rude!" Pan snapped. "They are right there!"

The guard's fly swatter froze mid-swing, and he sat up like a scolded schoolchild. Pan had a great way of acting over confident – nasty, even – in tricky situations. The guard nodded quickly and waved us through, even though the couple Pan claimed were our parents were Japanese tourists who looked about eighty.

I clambered onto some rocks and gazed across a sprawl of crumbled temples, half-standing columns and ruined villas. The ancient city sat in a valley, hugged by craggy slopes speckled with olive trees. Unlike the ruins in Rome, these had been *left* to ruin. There were no neat paths, no information plaques, and definitely no gift shop. Most of the ruins were overgrown with long grass and wild flowers. No one had tried to put the fallen columns back together, and mosaics had been left for tourists to walk over.

Actually there weren't many tourists left at the site. It was past dusk, and getting cold. A few solo travellers wandered amid the rubble, and a coach-load of sightseers seemed to be competing to take the most photos with the largest camera. Otherwise, there was an eerie silence to the place. It really felt like a frontier.

"So this was the edge of the Roman empire?" I asked.

Pan tried to hide a smile. I knew how much she enjoyed giving me history lessons. "No one really knows how the Romans decided the extent of their empire," she explained. "In some places natural barriers like rivers made good defences, so they stopped there. Or maybe they just decided it wasn't worth the hassle of fighting whichever tribes lived beyond that border."

"What about here?"

"Well, this was different. The Romans thought there was nothing else out there. This was as far west as they *wanted* to go."

"So what are we looking for?"

"We think Marcus Turbo's guards brought one of the keys here, right? So we need a clue to show us where they hid it."

I agreed, but this didn't feel right. Our parents had taught us to always have a plan, but we didn't really know what we were looking for. More than ever I wished they were there. Pan and I had been alone before on missions, and it never felt right. Despite all our squabbles, the Atlas family worked better together.

Luckily, Pan remembered we had a job to do. She jumped up beside me on the rocks and gazed in every direction. "The Praetorian Guards would have hidden the key somewhere discreet," she said. "Away from the busy areas of the town."

"What do we know about this place?" I asked.

I often said *we* when I meant *you*, and Pan was grateful for another opportunity to play teacher. She pointed down an avenue that ran between two huge triumphal arches. The road was lined on both sides with smaller arches, most of which had collapsed. "That was the town's high street," she said. "There were shops inside the arches."

"What about the ruins on either side of it?"

"Posh houses, where the rich lived. Maybe they hid the key there?"

She didn't sound convinced, and I wasn't either. The high street would have been too public. "What was beyond the street?" I asked. "Those columns over there."

"That was a temple," Pan replied. "Further on was the Forum, bathhouses and the basilica."

"That's even *more* public," I muttered.

"Well, there wasn't much else here other than the factories."

I looked at her, shielding my eyes from the dazzle of the setting sun. "Factories?"

Pan leaped down from the rocks. "Those ruins beyond the Forum were olive presses," she said. "Farmers made oil to send back to Rome."

I felt a tingle in my stomach, a gut-feeling I'd learned to trust...

"Let's check those," I said.

Pan called them factories, but each building was tiny. There were maybe a dozen square patches of rubble, each no bigger than a double bed, crammed together beyond the remains of the temple. Narrow paths wound between them, along which the Romans had rolled barrels of olives to press into oil. I stood for a moment, letting warm wind rustle against me, trying to imagine the scene. It must have been hot, dirty and...

"Busy," I thought aloud.

Here, everyone had been busy. No one would pay attention to anyone else. This area, more than any, seemed like a good place to be secretive.

"Pan, do you think the Praetorians came here in their fancy uniforms?"

"No way, they'd have been noticed. They were army superstars."

"So they came in disguise..."

"You mean as oil makers?"

I shrugged. It seemed possible. "Let's look around."

We set to it like hunting dogs, scurrying around the ruins, crouching to examine each stone in every ruined factory. It was tricky: the ruins were heavily overgrown with yellow and red wildflowers, so the factories looked more like flowerbeds than archaeological remains.

"Jake, look at this!"

I leaped over several ruins to joined Pan at the far end of the site, in the shadow of the city wall. She was on her hands and knees, tearing tufts of grass from the ground and brushing away the earth.

"There's a mosaic here, Jake!"

"So?"

"These were oil presses, not fancy homes. None of them should have had mosaics. Unless this was secretly something *other* than an oil press."

I got down beside her and we cleared away enough grass and earth to see the tiled image that filled half of the building's floor. Two thousand years of scorching wind and sunlight had reduced the picture to a faded outline, but we recognized it well enough. We should have, after all this time.

"The ouroboros," Pan breathed.

Frantically, we tore away more grass, exposing the

rest of the mosaic. I hoped to see some Latin writing, a clue to finding the next key, but there was nothing else there – just a black snake on a white square. Pan instructed her smart-goggles to zoom and examined the tiles up close, expecting to find some hidden message. Excitement turned to frustration as she continued scrabbling around the picture, scratching away dirt.

"There must be something else here..."

I slid my smart-goggles on too. *"Ultrasonic."*

My view in the lenses changed to an echolocation soundscape: graph pattern lines made by sound waves bouncing off empty spaces. I hoped it might reveal a secret chamber under the mosaic, but the ground beneath it was solid.

Pan sat back, cursing. "The Praetorians were here, Jake. So where did they hide the key?"

She grabbed a handful of grass and tore it angrily, and then another, cracking some of the tiles. I edged back, as if from a ticking bomb. Pan would never destroy antiquities unless she was really, *really*...

"Pan," I hissed. "Stop."

I had to repeat myself a few times until she heard. She rose, gazing at the mosaic; it was scattered with tufts of grass and tiles she'd dislodged in her rage.

"What?" she asked.

Something had caught my attention. That happened sometimes; my mind finds order in chaos... I crouched to examine one of the tiles Pan had broken, a piece no bigger than a postage stamp. It was white on one side, the background colour of the snake image, but it was blue on the other.

"Were these usually painted on both sides?" I asked.

Pan plucked the tile from my hand. "They shouldn't be. I mean, why would they be?"

I grabbed a sharp stone and used it to dig up another tile, and then another, flipping each one over.

"They're all painted on the other side," Pan said. Her eyes gleamed with renewed hope. "Maybe this isn't just a mosaic. Jake, maybe it's *two* mosaics."

"We need to turn every tile over," I said. "But keep each one in its exact place."

"There are thousands. It could take hours."

"Where else do we have to be?"

# 16

We worked in shifts, one of us keeping an eye on the guard at the site entrance, while the other used a stone to dig up mosaic tiles and carefully turn them over. It was frustratingly slow, but we couldn't speed up. If we broke one tile, or lost its place on the mosaic, we might ruin whatever secret was hidden underneath.

If there *was* a secret.

A few tourists wandered in our direction, but Pan shooed them away. If anyone caught us vandalizing the site they'd report us to the guard.

Actually the guard seemed more interested in his bottle of booze. After about an hour, he wrapped himself in a blanket and turned his Jeep's stereo on full blast for company during his lonely shift. By then the sun had sunk low over the site, colouring its columns neon pink and orange. Storks settled in nests on top of arches. Scared of being seen, we used the night vision setting on our goggles, as the wind rustling among the ruins grew colder.

And colder.

At first, the chill was a relief from the relentless heat of the day. But as the sky darkened and stars lit up over the hills, the temperature continued to drop. By nine o'clock, my fingers trembled so hard that it was tricky to hold the tiles, and my curses came out in frozen clouds. We couldn't move much to keep warm for fear of being seen. After another hour, the idea of being caught didn't seem so bad. The guard would arrest us, and we could sit in his nice warm Jeep...

"This is awful," Pan mumbled. "We're going to die here."

By eleven o'clock, I could barely lift the tiles. Only one thing kept me from marching to the guard and turning myself in: with each new tile, we grew more certain that there was something under the mosaic.

It was past midnight when we turned the final piece. Pan set it in its place, and we leaned over the mosaic. Our goggles' gritty-green night-vision filter made it impossible to see much detail, but there was definitely a pattern. But if we used the torch to see it, the guard would notice...

"So what now?" Pan whispered.

"Can you still drive?" I asked.

She looked anxiously towards the guard and his

Jeep. "I think so," she muttered. "Why?"

Our parents had taught us loads of skills to use on missions, including driving. I'd never got the hang of it, but Pan had.

"OK," I explained, "we'll light a torch and take a photo of this mosaic with our goggles. The guard will see and rush over. We circle around, swipe his Jeep, and go."

Pan nodded, but she didn't look convinced. "The guard has a gun, Jake. He'll think we're stealing his Jeep."

"We *would* be stealing it."

"I know, and he's got a gun!"

"Pan, without this clue we'll never find the next key or save Mum and Dad."

She looked away, pulling her shirt tighter against the biting cold. "Jake, maybe *that's* the best plan. Not to do this. We made a promise, remember? It was the last thing Dad said."

I didn't feel the cold then, just anger – a sudden and intense heat, as if someone had set fire to my insides. How could Pan ask if I remembered? I'd been there, I'd seen the smoke take them. But I was never going to keep that promise we made. I couldn't. We couldn't.

"Pan, we have to forget that."

"Jake, it was the only thing he ever asked of us."

"I know," I hissed. "I know that! But he shouldn't have, and we shouldn't have agreed. We're going to save them, Pan. I'll do it alone if you won't."

She sighed, and cursed under her breath. "Don't be stupid. That'd be even worse." She slid her smart-goggles back on. "OK, get ready."

Before I could reply, she whispered *"Torch"*, causing a super-lumen beam to shine from her goggles onto the tiles. The light dazzled me after so long in the dark, so I didn't get a proper look. I glimpsed shapes, green and brown and blue, and Latin writing...

Then, a shout.

Another torch bobbed closer. The guard was coming.

Pan took a photo, then yanked me away. "Let's go!"

We got down low and scurried around the edge of the site, using night vision to keep an eye on the guard. He seemed scared, waggling his rifle in the air and shouting. I didn't blame him. He had no idea who was lurking in the dark.

We reached his Jeep and clambered into the front. The seats trembled from the volume of the music blaring from the stereo. I had to shout to be heard, as Pan fumbled with the key.

"Drive!" I cried.

She pumped the pedals and yanked at the gear stick. "Stupid old banger..."

I wiped dirt from my eyes and looked back across the site. "He's coming!" I yelped. "Can you just drive?"

"I'm trying, obviously!"

A loud crack rang across the night, and we sank down in the seats.

"What was that?" Pan shrieked.

"The car backfired. Just get it going!"

Actually, the guard had fired his rifle, but Pan needed to concentrate, so I kept that to myself...

She stamped on the accelerator. The Jeep lurched forward and stalled. Another gunshot hit the ground a few metres away, spraying up dirt. The guard was getting closer...

"Pan..."

"I'm trying, Jake!"

"Pan!"

She glared at me with wild, terrified eyes.

"Breathe," I said.

For a second, she released the controls. She breathed in, held her breath for a second, and let it go. Then she started to drive.

We swerved away from the guard, screaming as he fired again and again. I don't know if he was a bad shot or too drunk to aim, but none of the bullets hit the car as Pan steered us from the dirt track and onto the road.

We drove as fast as we could with the windscreen covered with dust.

"Did you get the photo?" I gasped.

Pan shifted in her seat, struggling to see through the only patch of glass that wasn't smeared with dirt. "I think so," she replied. "What if it's nothing, Jake?"

I didn't reply; we just had to hope.

We drove for another hour, following signs to Fez. The adrenaline from stealing the Jeep wore off, and Pan looked on the verge of falling asleep at the wheel. We finally stopped a few miles outside Fez and parked behind a barn full of bleating goats. We needed to rest, but neither of us felt like sleeping. Not until we'd seen the photo.

Pan pulled her smart-goggles from her pocket. She glanced at me, her face ghostly pale and eyes full of worry. We should have been excited, but I felt like I was about to bungee jump from a bridge. So much depended on one hastily snapped photograph. What if it was too blurry to see? What if there was *nothing* to see?

"Well, here we go," Pan said. She slid the goggles on. "Show last photograph."

She stared into the lenses for what seemed like an eternity, as light from the image glimmered off her eyes.

"Well?" I asked, unable to stand the suspense. "Do you see anything?"

The edge of her mouth curled into a slight smile, just a twitch of a muscle. Trying not to give anything away, she pulled off the goggles and handed them to me.

I gazed at the photograph, unaware I was holding my breath until my lungs ached, and I exhaled in a long, relieved sigh. Even in the harsh light of Pan's torch, and after 2000 years, the upturned mosaic – the *hidden* mosaic – was brilliantly clear. It showed mountains, a desert and Latin writing.

"It's a map," I breathed.

"Not just any map, brother. It's a treasure map." Pan lost her fight against the smile, which spread wide and beaming across her face. "We're back in business."

# 17

*The black smoke.*

*Like a monstrous slug, it slid closer.*

*I scrabbled back as rocks cascaded down mountainsides, smashing houses to rubble. People with dark skin and shaved heads fled the chaos, their white tunics torn and splattered with blood. This wasn't just an earthquake. In the distance, waves crashed against the sides of the pyramid. A tsunami.*

*The smoke drifted closer. From inside I heard my parents screaming my name. I backed into something hard and turned, astonished, to see a door set into the base of a cliff.*

*Twenty metres away, the smoke had stopped. I sensed it was letting me stand, letting me see this door.*

*The door was made of thick, green stone – emerald, I thought, like the tablets we'd found in the tombs of the lost civilization. Set into it were four crystal keys, each with hundreds of gleaming cogs. The keys were throbbing, like hearts beating.*

*The smoke moved again.*

*It drifted closer. A face began to form in its darkness, those black-hole eyes and the grinning mouth that I'd seen before. As the grin widened, another voice screamed from inside the smoke. A single cry, but the most desperate and pained yet.*

*"Pan?" I gasped.*

I woke, bolt upright and soaked with sweat. The dream had disorientated me. I was in a Jeep. Was I in Rome? No, the windows were misted, but I heard goats bleating and remembered where we'd parked last night. Pan lay across the back seats with her hood pulled over her head and her raven-black fringe flopping into her eyes. She clutched the backpack with the two keys, like a toddler with a favourite teddy bear. My head throbbed from dehydration and my back ached from my awkward sleeping position. I was about to go outside to stretch and look for water, but Pan spoke.

"Jake?"

I looked back. She was still curled up like she was fast asleep, but now I wondered if she'd really slept at all.

"Do you remember our promise to Dad?" she asked.

I yawned, stretching out a crick in my neck. "You mean about brushing our teeth?"

"No, Jake."

Of course I knew what she meant, but I didn't want to talk about it. This past year we'd thrown ourselves into all sorts of dangers, but Mum and Dad had never suggested we should leave them behind. This time, though, Dad feared that if we came after them we would die. I'd seen it in his eyes when he spoke to us.

"We promised him, Jake," Pan repeated softly.

I nodded slowly and opened the Jeep door. "We're going to have to break that promise," I said.

I let Pan rest for a while, but eventually a farmer came and yelled at us for parking near his goats. We drove on for a mile or so and dumped the Jeep behind another barn. From there we walked the last few miles to Fez.

We needed to talk about the map we'd found, but for the next hour Fez demanded our full attention. It was a crazy place. A high wall wrapped around the town's medieval quarter – a *medina* – which was as close to a maze as anything that isn't actually a maze.

Covered alleys spread in a tangle up a hill, twisting and criss-crossing. Some turned into tunnels, dipping under buildings and popping back up. Others were crammed with stalls selling fruit so shiny it looked plastic, chickens crammed into cages, or strange combinations of goods: bananas and leather gloves, copper pots and candles, woven carpets and fly swatters. Butchers hacked at slabs of meat as hopeful cats licked their lips. The place felt like a movie set, a big-budget blockbuster set in the Middle Ages. There were no cars or scooters; people rode donkeys and mules, barking at us to move aside as they steered the beasts past.

It stank, too. Some places, like back home in England, don't smell of anything. The stenches are washed away by efficient drains or banned by health inspectors. But exciting places attack your nose at every turn. Some of Fez's smells were great: fried fish, grilled meat, fresh mint tea. Others were not: donkey poo, open sewers, the acrid reek of the tannery, where workers plunged leather hides into buckets of cat pee and pigeon poo. But not one thing was dull. I loved places like this.

I'm not proud of what we did next. Another survival skill our parents taught us was pickpocketing. We'd promised it was only for emergencies, and this seemed to fit that description – we needed food, and Fez's crowded alleys were perfect for "accidentally" bumping into people to swipe a wallet. The first one Pan stole was empty, but I got lucky with the second, which was crammed with local currency. We kept its ID card too, so we could repay the owner once this was over.

Then we sat at a rooftop cafe scoffing cheese omelettes, semolina pancakes covered in honey and hot, crispy Moroccan doughnuts called *sfenj*, as we gazed across the medina's scruffy skyline – a patchwork of rooftops, square minaret towers, and multi-coloured washing hung out to dry. Around us, locals played backgammon, sipping super-sweet mint tea.

We were supposed to be resting, but every muscle in my body was tense, like I'd been put in a torture device.

I kept thinking about the dream.

The ancient people, the crystal door... Were they things that the smoke – whatever that was – had wanted me to see? That thought rang around my head, causing it to ache. If the smoke wanted to stop us collecting the keys, why did it send us here, where we could find one? Unless it *wanted* us to find them.

Was it using us?

Even if we did find all four keys, we didn't yet know how to use them to save Mum and Dad. But we had a mission. One of Mum's lessons was to make a plan and stick to it. Well, we had to. Not least because we didn't have any *other* plan.

"Are we even sure the mosaic is a map?" I asked.

"Definitely," Pan confirmed.

She slid on her goggles to study the photograph. "This label identifies Volubilis. The rest of the map shows mountains to the south, but it only names one of them. Look..."

She handed me the goggles. I recognized the name of Volubilis on the map, written inside a circle of city walls. The other label was at the bottom, a word I didn't know below a blood-coloured mountain shaped like a pyramid with its top chopped off.

"What does it say under that mountain?" I asked.

"It translates as tower of fire," Pan explained.

"So that's the name of this mountain?"

"Maybe it was its Roman name, but all those mountains have Arabic names now. I searched, and none are called tower of fire, or anything like that."

She'd already searched? So she hadn't slept much last night, after all. It showed in her face, which was even paler than usual, and her eyes looked sore and red. I wished we had more time to rest, but the People of the Snake had found the chamber under Rome, and probably the mosaic at Volubilis, too. We'd been in such a rush to get away we'd not thought to destroy that clue. If they weren't already ahead of us, they would be soon.

"So why did the Romans call it that?" I asked. "Weird name for a mountain. Unless..."

Pan snatched the goggles from my face, and gave them another command. *"Show locations of volcanoes in Morocco."*

I shifted closer, trying to catch a glimpse inside the lenses.

*"Satellite view,"* Pan instructed. *"Zoom in on left quadrant. Discard. Zoom in on the middle. Zoom closer."*

She took the goggles off and grinned. *"Jbel Sirwa,"* she said. "It's an extinct volcano, about an eight-hour drive south. That's where the Romans took the third key. They wanted to get it as far from Volubilis as possible, beyond the edge of their empire and into the mountains."

"So that's where we go," I said.

Pan frowned. "Because it's always that simple?"

"You never know, sis, maybe this time it will be. But not unless we eat more of these doughnuts, and get some supplies."

I looked at her until she understood.

"It's my turn to steal the next wallet, isn't it?" she asked.

"Get a big one, I'm starving."

# 18

Even with our stolen cash, it was tricky to find a taxi driver to take us south. Two kids travelling alone, stinking of sewage, with only a backpack and matching sunglasses... We had to offer double the fare, and even then the driver kept asking about our parents. Eventually Pan snapped at the poor guy for being rude, although he wasn't. He turned up the air conditioning and put on some music for the long journey.

Pan pulled her hood over her head and had a nap, knowing we'd need as much rest as we could get. I didn't want to sleep; I was scared to. I feared the dreams of the black smoke, the destruction, of Pan screaming my name...

I leaned my head against the window, watching the landscape slowly change from rippled hills scattered with fields and farm houses to stark, rust-coloured mountains. It looked like the surface of

Mars, still and silent. The only life I saw were vultures with wings as big as surfboards, swooping over high, craggy ridges. I imagined Marcus Turbo and his Praetorians carrying the key beyond the border of their empire. They must have felt pretty far from home. I know I did.

The further south we drove, the hotter it became. The taxi's air conditioning blasted out icy air, so we were actually cold in the car, but I could see the heat outside. The sky was a hazy blue, and mirages shimmered on the road ahead. We'd forgotten to buy suncream. Mum would kill us if she knew.

I pressed my head harder against the glass. "Mum," I whispered. "Where are you?"

We were breaking Dad's promise more with every passing hour. But I forced the thought from my mind, listening instead to Mum's voice in my head. *You make a plan and you stick to it.* Find the mountain, find the key.

I just wished we'd brought suncream...

In the end I was too tired not to fall asleep, but this time there were no dreams. I woke with my head against the taxi window and sweat stinging my eyes. The air con must have broken because it felt as if I'd woken up in an oven. One of my arms was stuck with sweat to the leather seat, which was as hot as a frying pan. The taxi had just swerved from an overtaking truck that had almost barged us off the road. Our driver cursed as another truck roared past, sending up such a cloud of dust that he was forced to pull over.

The driver honked his horn, but the trucks didn't care, as they clattered along the road. I rubbed my eyes, wiping away sweat and sleep to see through the dust. In an instant I was wide awake.

I reached for my backpack and pulled out my smart-goggles.

*"Zoom,"* I said.

The lenses gave me a close-up view of the trucks. They were identical: black, military-looking, with canvas covers hiding their cargo.

"Army," the taxi driver grunted.

"No," I said, "not army."

I pulled off the goggles and gave Pan a shake.

She growled at me from under her hood. "What?"

"They're here," I replied.

It took her a few seconds to process the reply, and then she sat up and tossed back her hood. Her eyes were suddenly sharp as she stared through the windshield at the vehicles speeding away.

"The People of the Snake," she hissed. "They're here."

"Only three trucks," I said, trying to sound optimistic.

Right then a helicopter flew over us, so low that its downdraft caused the taxi to jolt. Our driver didn't get time to curse before several more military 'copters swept overhead. At the same time another convoy of trucks rushed past on the road.

"Twelve trucks and six helicopters," Pan counted. "And two of us."

"With no suncream," I muttered.

"Suncream? Jake, they have an army. Where are we, anyway?"

"Close to Atougha," the driver replied.

Atougha was a village at the foot of Jbel Sirwa, where we'd told the driver our parents were waiting. I felt sure the People of the Snake would use it as their base to find the key. We needed to get there too; it was the only settlement close to Jbel Sirwa, and we needed more water if we hoped to climb the mountain in this heat.

Obviously we couldn't just rock up in the town square; we'd have to sneak in on foot. We told the taxi driver we needed a walk, but he wasn't too happy about leaving us by the road. In the end we gave him a huge tip and he finally drove off, leaving us alone in the scorching desert.

Our direction was simple, even without smart-goggles. Jbel Sirwa wasn't only higher than the other mountains around it, but its red was deeper too, nearly the colour of blood. Actually, it looked almost like two mountains, one plonked on top of the other. Its lower slopes rose gently enough for us to hike up – if we could get past the People of the Snake. I prayed we'd find a clue to the next key somewhere there, because I didn't think we could get any higher. Halfway up, the mountain suddenly rose into brutally steep rock faces, rising like the sides of a pyramid to a jagged summit. We'd studied satellite images of the mountain on our smart-goggles, so we knew that the summit wasn't really a summit. In fact, it was the jagged ridge of a volcanic crater, like a huge funnel, on the other side.

Luckily Jbel Sirwa was an *extinct* volcano. The whole region was parched and eerily lifeless.

From the road we could see the village at the mountain's base: a scruffy collection of farmhouses, barns and a mosque with a spear-like minaret. The People of the Snake must have quadrupled the village's population. Our goggles' zoom lenses picked out an operations tent, satellite dishes and a dozen mercenaries unloading trucks. It looked like they were about to go to war against the mountain.

"Come on," Pan said.

We scrambled down a slope and made our way cross-country, hiding behind rocks each time a helicopter took off from the village. Several had set off on missions to search the mountain, but there were other things in the air too, much smaller machines that hovered above the slopes like bees around a nest. I had another look with my smart-goggles.

"Jetpacks," I muttered. "That's pretty cool."

A dozen or so mercenaries were strapped into super-high-tech gadgets with fuel tanks and tiny carbon wings. I guessed the machines were kitted out with scanning cameras too. The People of the

Snake were hoping to get lucky and find a secret chamber, or something, to lead them to the key. But it would take them days to search the whole mountain. Maybe we had time to find it first. Only we didn't know where to look either...

"We'll have to go around the village," Pan suggested. "Hopefully we can find a way onto the mountain from the other side."

"No, we should go into the village," I replied. "We need water and suncream."

"Jake, I'm not risking my life for suncream."

"Mum says that's the number one rule of—"

"I don't care what she says. We can do without suncream, and we can find water somewhere on—"

"There's other stuff we need."

"Like what?"

"Well, sun hats. And lunch would be good. Oh, and we need to sabotage those helicopters, blow up whatever tech they have in those tents and disable their satellite communication, probably by blowing that up as well."

She stared at me, processing what I had just blurted.

I shrugged. "But suncream too."

# 19

We sneaked to Atougha and broke into the first building we reached, a farmhouse with stone walls and a corrugated iron roof. The window was high and tiny, so it took a few minutes for me to scramble up and squeeze through it with my backpack, then reach down to help Pan in too. Any noise we made was drowned out by the constant *whump, whump, whump* of helicopters taking off and landing on the other side of the village, and – much closer by – the rocket roar of jetpack fuel burners as mercenaries flew off on missions to search the mountain for the Praetorians' hidden key.

The house was empty. The People of the Snake had forced every villager into a truck and driven them away, barking about gas leaks and emergency evacuations. Safe inside, we filled our water bottles and scoffed bread from a counter, and then searched for anything else that might help our mission.

I crept up a rickety staircase to a bedroom. As I stepped inside, the floorboards shuddered and something rattled the window. I peeled back a curtain and peeked out, and almost cried out, my stomach somersaulting with fright. I'd known our enemies were close, but not *that* close.

The People of the Snake had pitched their operations tent about fifty metres away, in a square outside the village mosque. Its canvas flaps were pinned back, and I spotted at least twenty mercenaries inside working on holospheres or examining satellite images and 3D projections of Jbel Sirwa. I could make out the lanky figure of Lord Osthwait, leaning on his cane and still wrapped in his huge fur coat despite the heat.

Beyond, a helicopter rigged with high-tech scanning kit took off on a mission to search the mountain. Between the tent and this house, the mercenaries had set up six charging docks for their jetpacks – generators with dozens of wires snaking in and out, and screens giving complicated readings. One of them was right outside the house, where a jetpack mercenary had just landed. I watched as the pilot unstrapped the pack and slotted it into the charging dock. He hung a helmet on a rack and rushed off to the operations tent to deliver his report.

I stared at the jetpack, trying to resist the idea that was invading my head.

"Don't do it," I whispered. "Don't be dumb..."

I rushed downstairs to the front door. Pan was shoving a few things from around the house into my backpack with the keys. "I got water, bread and some goat cheese that may be rotten," she announced. "You find anything?"

I opened the door carefully and peered out.

"Maybe," I muttered.

I was trying to hide it, but Pan had a way of knowing when I was planning something crazy.

"Oh, God," she said. "Why are you grinning like that?"

"Come on," I whispered.

I darted to the jetpack. Pan joined me a second later with the backpack. We were well hidden behind the docking generator, but I suspected the mercenaries would be back soon, so we didn't have much time. I examined the pack on its dock, trying to work the machine out.

"Wait," Pan said, "you're not going to use *that*, are you?"

"*We*," I replied.

"Eh?"

"*We* are going to use it."

"No way. Jake, *absolutely* no way."

"It will get us onto the mountain, Pan."

"Are you mad? We have no idea how to fly it. And there's only one."

"But it carried a big guy. I reckon it will hold us both."

Pan kept protesting, but I stopped listening as I examined the machine up close. It was powered by some sort of mega-energy fuel core, which a screen on the generator indicated was only a quarter charged. There were buttons on the frame, and a joystick on its arm for steering. The pilot sat in a perch, kept in by straps that I was reasonably confident would hold me and Pan...

I stepped up onto the platform and slid into the pilot seat. I felt the machine's power immediately. It throbbed, like a living thing.

"Jake, five mercenaries are coming this way fast."

"Hold them off, this thing's not charged."

"What do you mean *hold them off*?"

"There's a stun gun there. Shoot at them."

"Shoot at them? What if I hit them?"

"It's a stun gun, Pan."

"I don't approve of *any* guns."

"Can you change your policy on that for two minutes?"

"Not really. Principles are important. Not that you'd understand about–"

"Don't aim at them. Just fire in the air."

"What if I hit a bird?"

"Pan!"

"OK, OK!"

Despite her disapproval, Pan had actually used a stun gun before, so she didn't need to work it out. She just grabbed it and started firing. She was a great shot, too. Mercenaries shrieked and scuttled for cover behind a goat pen as they came under surprise attack by fizzing blue blasts of electricity.

"Jake!" Pan screamed.

I cursed under my breath – the pack was still less than half charged. Was that enough? At least it might get us away from there.

"Let's go!" I yelled.

Pan fired a final shot, and then dropped the stun gun and ran to me.

"Get on my lap," I said. "I'll strap us in."

"Your *lap*?"

"It'll carry us both, I'm sure."

"How sure? You literally just saw this thing for the first time."

"I'm reasonably confident."

"You're risking our lives on *reasonably confident*? What about those helmets? Do we need those?"

"Nah."

We definitely needed those helmets, but we were out of time. Boots stomped closer as the mercenaries approached. Swearing at me, Pan climbed up from the crate and sat on my lap, clutching the backpack to her chest. I fastened the straps around us, securing us in the seat.

"You ready?" I called.

"No!" Pan wailed.

"Great!"

I don't know what I expected to happen when

I pressed the ignition. Maybe a gentle rumble, like a kettle boiling, followed by a slow take-off while I worked out the controls. I didn't like that idea – we'd be target practice for the mercenaries – but I liked what really happened even less.

A jet of fire blasted from the fuel tank, and we shot into the air as if we'd been flung from a catapult. We didn't stop screaming until we were fifty metres high, and only then because our mouths dried up from the rush of air.

I lifted my thumb off the ignition and we dropped straight down towards the generator. I slammed my thumb back on the button. Another blast from the fuel tank shot us even higher – a hundred metres above the village – and Pan almost dropped the backpack. She pulled it even tighter to her chest, screaming curses at me.

Crackling blue streaks shot past us as the mercenaries below opened fire.

"Get us out of here!" Pan yelled.

# 20

Mum once told me that on each new mission I would learn something new about myself. Well, right then I learned that I was really bad at flying jetpacks.

I tilted the joystick and we shot off to our left. I nudged it in the other direction and we flew fiercely to the right. Each thrust slammed us against the jet-pack's frame, like we were on a fairground ride. But after a few more zigzags and a lot more screaming, mad panic settled into bad flying. We were out of range of the stun guns, moving in stuttered bursts above the lower slopes of Jbel Sirwa.

"This is going pretty well," I shouted.

"Why did you say that?" Pan snapped. "Whenever you say that something goes wrong!"

I pressed the ignition again. The pack carried us up towards the mountain's higher, steeper cliff faces. "We're well ahead of them now," I insisted. "We can land and hunt for the key. What can go wrong?"

"Now, why did you say *that*?"

Another thrust fired us forward, which was weird because I hadn't pressed the ignition. Something had pushed us from behind. I glanced over my shoulder and shrieked.

We'd been pushed by an updraft. From a helicopter.

The People of the Snake were coming after us in a helicopter rigged with something that looked worryingly like an electrolaser cannon...

"Uh, Pan?"

"Don't tell me," she cried.

"But–"

"I don't want to know!"

The laser cannon fired a blue lightning bolt that singed the hairs on my arm even though it missed us by ten metres.

"Why, Jake?" Pan hollered. "Why does this always happen? Is this treasure hunting?"

It was the only type of treasure hunting that I knew; we were always up to stupid stuff like this. Well, maybe not *this* stupid.

"Get us out of here!" Pan demanded again.

I pressed the ignition and tilted the joystick so we shot upwards with another blast from the jet-pack's fuel tank. Hot wind whipped at our faces as we rushed up one of Jbel Sirwa's rock faces, startling a flock of starlings from a ledge. The helicopter was coming after us still but it was unable to match our speed as we rose towards the mountain's summit.

"Ha!" I yelled. "Keep up with *that*!"

"Jake, look out!"

I yanked the joystick, thrusting us to the side just as a second helicopter rose from the other side of the mountain and fired its stun cannon. The shot missed, but now the first helicopter fired from behind. We flew straight up, so high we could see over the jagged mountain ridge to the funnel-shaped volcanic crater on the other side. One of the helicopters came after us as the other lay in wait below.

"Jake!" Pan hollered. "You were certain this was safe!"

"*Reasonably* certain, I said! Just hold on..."

I released the ignition so the fuel tank cut out. We dropped thirty metres, then I hit the button again and rammed the joystick forward so we flew right under the lower helicopter. The other pilot anticipated the dodge and swooped to cut us off. It fired a laser shot, then several more. I swerved from side to side, only just avoiding the electrolaser blasts. Soon one of those shots would find its target.

"Stop moving around so much!" Pan snapped.

"I'm dodging laser blasts!"

I swerved again, flying in erratic bursts to confuse the pilots as we rose again towards the summit ridge.

A red light started flashing on the jetpack. That was not a good sign on any machine, let alone one on which your lives depended.

"I think we're running out of fuel."

"Get us down!" Pan insisted.

There were now mercenaries all over the slope below, like ants around a nest. If we landed we'd be caught – and they'd get the keys.

The light blinked faster. I didn't know how much time we had, but I guessed not much...

"Jake, we have to land."

We were a few metres from the cliff, facing both helicopters. Their laser cannons swivelled and found us in their sights. A ball of blue fire gathered at their ends. They were about to shoot... Then something *really* strange happened.

The helicopters vanished.

"*What the...?*" I gasped.

Pan said nothing. She sat in front of me, motionless, as if she'd passed out.

"Pan?" I called. "What's going on?"

The sky darkened. Black clouds rolled over the mountain ridge, blocking the sun. No, I realized, not black clouds.

Black smoke.

It tumbled and spread, spilling over the mountain like a vast ink stain.

Behind us, something moved.

Five figures scrambled up the slope. Their white tunics were torn and covered in dirt, but it was the sandals that I really noticed.

*Calcei* not *caligae*.

It was the Praetorian Guard. I was watching a scene from over two thousand years ago, as if it was happening right then. Only it didn't feel *entirely* real. My mind was foggy, like it had been in the dreams of the destruction of the lost civilization. But I was awake. I felt the sun bake my neck, tasted salt from the sweat on my face and heard the roar of the jetpack as I tilted the joystick to follow the Romans. They shuffled along a ledge of a rock wall that rose to the rim of the volcano crater. Without hesitating they began to climb. If one of them slipped, he'd drop thirty metres to the slope below. But none of them looked fazed by the danger. Their arms were rippled with muscles, burned by the sun and criss-crossed with scratches and old battle scars. Some of the wounds had come open, and blood soaked with sweat into the ragged remains of their tunics.

Each man carried a small pack that was lashed to his back with a leather strap. But one had a second bag; a leather satchel slung over his shoulder. I noticed him touch it, making sure its contents hadn't fallen out.

The key was in that bag.

And that man, I felt certain, was Marcus Turbo.

He was shorter and slimmer than the other Praetorians, but he looked tougher than them all. His nose was flat and a livid scar ran across his cheek from his ear to his mouth, shining like a beacon in the fierce sun.

He moved faster than the other soldiers too. Halfway up the climb, he leaped to grab a rock. Had he missed he would have died for sure. But there was a confidence to his movements, like he'd done this a dozen times. His speed and courage inspired the others; they gritted their teeth and battled to keep up. They helped one another to the crater top, and even then they didn't rest.

"They're taking the key down into the crater," I whispered.

One of the soldiers pulled a rope from his pack and tossed one end into the crater. He tied the other end around a rock and tested it to take his weight. But, again, it was Turbo who led the way. Grabbing the rope, he scrambled over the ridge and abseiled into the crater, headed towards a dark hole at its base: the volcano's core.

He stopped, and touched his satchel again, as if he'd forgotten – or remembered – something. He glanced down, then all around him. The scar on his face crinkled as he frowned.

Then he looked up – at me.

His glare was like a spear of ice, freezing my insides. I'd fought trained mercenaries and some seriously tough treasure hunters, but I'd never felt anything like the threat I sensed from that look. I wanted to fly away, but Turbo's stare was like a force, a traction beam trapping me in the sky. As I hovered above him, staring, wisps of black smoke drifted from Turbo's eyes.

"Jake!"

Daylight dazzled me. I blinked, and it was all gone – the smoke, the Romans. I was back in the present. Pan was screaming. The helicopters flew closer, about to fire their lasers. The red light flashed on the jetpack, and the machine shuddered so hard that my teeth clacked together.

"Jake..." Pan gasped.

"Pan, you trust me, right?"

"No!"

"Come on, of course you do."

"I don't, especially now. Don't do anything stupid!"

I pressed the ignition and slammed the joystick forward, so we shot up and away from the helicopters with a spluttering thrust from the fuel tank. The flashing light cut out, and the roar of the jetpack was replaced by a rush of wind as we rose ... and then began to fall.

I glanced down, praying I'd judged this right.

The pack had carried us over the ridge, so we were falling towards the crater slope on the other side, a twenty-metre plunge that would have broken our legs had the jetpack been completely out of fuel...

I pressed the ignition just before we hit the slope and the machine gave one last splutter, a jet *cough* rather than a jet *blast.* It was enough to lift us a few metres, a jolt that felt like it ripped my spine from my back. Then we fell the final few metres to the crater slope.

We landed hard. I unclipped the straps and we tumbled from the jetpack. Only, what now? I'd hoped the slope would break our fall, but I had no plan for once we landed.

We started to slide.

I tried to dig my feet into the ground, but I was moving too fast. Beside me, Pan slid head-first down the slope, screaming the whole way. My backpack whacked me on the head, and then the jetpack hit me much harder as they both tumbled past, headed – like us – towards the pit at the crater's base. And we had no idea how deep that pit was...

Tiny rocks shot up from the slope. One struck the side of my eye, and my world turned crimson as blood filled my vision. I was just able to see the jet-pack vanish into the crater hole. A plan came to me, but it went against every survival instinct.

I was trying to stop my slide, but really I needed to go *faster.*

Another rock hit my face. I tried to ignore the pain, clamping my legs together like I was on a water slide. I overtook Pan and then my backpack, flipped over and drove my toes into the scree surface, and my hands too, turning them into claws. At last I began to slow down, until I finally stopped a few feet up from the pit. I recovered fast enough to grab the backpack before it shot past, but Pan was still sliding, rushing right at me.

"Jaaaaaake!" she cried.

I shifted to the side and dug my feet deeper into the slope. Reaching out, I grabbed Pan's outstretched arm as she passed.

"Got you!" I grunted.

But with a lurch of horror, I realized that I hadn't. I tried to grip her wrist, but my fingers stung from the rocks and I let go. All I could do was watch as she plummeted into the pit.

# 21

I lay against the warm rock of the crater slope, my chest heaving.

"Pan..." I gasped.

All I heard was the frantic beating of my heart, and the *whump-whump* of rotors as the helicopters hovered over the crater. I screamed her name again and again, more desperate with each cry. Had I lost her? No, she might be alive. I had to get down there.

My hands shook so hard I almost slipped as I shifted down to the hole. I strapped the backpack over my shoulder and swung my legs into the pit, feeling for a foothold. Suddenly, something grabbed my ankle. I shrieked and kicked out, but the grip tightened, tugging me down harder and harder until I tumbled into the pit.

I dropped ten feet and landed on rock, knocking the wind from my body. The hand grabbed my arm.

Instinct kicked in and I swivelled around, swinging a leg. But the person anticipated the attack, jumping my kick and then twisting my arm behind my back.

"Stop fighting, you idiot!"

I wiped dirt, blood and sweat from my eyes and saw my sister silhouetted against the circle of sunlight that blazed into the pit.

"You're alive?" I wheezed.

"No thanks to you," she spat.

I rose on shaky legs, feeling my pockets for my smart-goggles. I slid them on and gave them an order.

*"Torch."*

The pit was barely five metres across, its walls covered with cracks, like shattered glass. One area, though, had been smoothed and covered with plaster – a narrow strip from the top of the pit to its base, on which the Praetorians had carved hundreds of lines of Latin inscription. They had dug a small niche into the wall, a space no bigger than a shoebox. Something sat inside.

"It's the key," Pan breathed.

Even covered in dust, it gleamed fiercely in the torchlight. For a moment we forgot about the helicopters swarming overhead and just stared. Was it really possible that this small artefact was the secret to saving the world?

We knew better than to just grab it. The Praetorians had feared this thing and tried to get it as far from

Rome as possible. They wouldn't have wanted it falling into the hands of their enemies.

I stepped back, guiding my torchlight around the ground. The floor looked like stone slabs slotted together, plugging the pit. It was obviously part of a trap. My guess was that the moment we lifted the key the slabs would fall away, taking us with them.

"We need a rock," I said. "Something the same weight as the key, to replace it with."

Pan ignored me, running a finger over the inscriptions. "We should read these," she muttered. "There's one more key to find, remember?"

"Take photos," I suggested. "We can look later."

"You know we can't do that."

She was right, of course. We were trapped in the pit, with our enemies at the top. They'd catch us now for sure. They'd take our smart-goggles, see any photos we took and use them to locate the next key. If there was a clue here, we needed to find it and then destroy it.

Pan's hands moved faster over the letters. She stopped, studying a particular line. "Jake," she breathed. "I think this is it..."

Silhouettes appeared at the top of the pit, black against the sun. The mercenaries were here. They raised their stun guns, making sure we could see the weapons.

"Jake and Pandora Atlas," one of them barked, "surrender or we will open fire."

"We *have* surrendered, you morons," I yelled. "We're stuck here and you're up there."

"And why are you raising your guns?" Pan added. "You can hardly miss us."

"Raise your hands and get down on your knees!"

"No," Pan replied.

"Do it now!"

"She said *no*," I insisted. "This is what's going to happen: you'll drop a rope and we'll climb up. We want a helicopter airlift, as well as water and food."

"Good food," Pan added. "And I'm a vegetarian."

"And I'd love a Coke," I shouted. "Not a can, a *bottle* of coke. A *glass* bottle. But listen..." I shaded my eyes, squinting to see them against the sunlight. "Are you listening? OK, this is important. *No Diet Coke*. That stuff is gross. Should someone be taking notes?"

They stared, dumbfounded.

"We're going to open fire now," one of them said.

"No, you're not," I shot back. "Let me tell you why. Actually, Pan, you tell them. I'm doing a lot of the talking."

"Thanks, brother," she said. She smiled at me, and then scowled at the mercenaries.

"None of you are going to shoot because we've read these inscriptions and you haven't. We know the location of the fourth key and you don't. We also know that the key down here is rigged to a weight trap."

She looked at me. "Jake?"

I reached into the niche and grabbed the key. The moment I lifted the artefact, the pit walls began to tremble.

"We just triggered the trap," Pan explained. "This pit is going to collapse, along with these inscriptions and three of the keys. So are you going to drop your rope, and do what we asked?"

"Don't forget the Coke," I added.

The pit floor shook harder. I shoved the key into my bag with the others and staggered back, as chunks of rock dislodged from the walls. Part of the ground fell away – one of the pieces of the stone jigsaw on which we'd been standing. I glimpsed a long drop into the volcano's core and felt hot air rush from the darkness. We pressed against one of the shaking walls as more of the jigsaw dropped into the abyss. Half of the floor was already gone; we only had seconds left until the rest fell away, taking us with it.

"Hey, you goons!" Pan screamed. "Do you really want to tell Lord Osthwait that you lost the keys *and* the next clue?"

Finally, the end of a rope dropped from above. We both grabbed hold just as the last piece of the floor fell into darkness.

We clung on as the mercenaries' gloved hands hoisted us up to the crater surface. Someone tore the backpack from my shoulder and threw us to the slope, as the others stood around us aiming stun guns. They were all shouting, so it was hard to make out any particular commands. I think one of them yelled "Get down on the ground!" which seemed a bit stupid, considering.

I picked myself up, trying not to look as terrified as I felt. They had the keys, but only Pan had seen the clue in the pit. Maybe we had something to bargain with...

"Look," I said, wiping dirt from my face, "maybe we can talk about–"

One of the mercenaries, a woman with a shaved undercut and a spider tattoo on her neck, grabbed my arm and dragged me to the edge of the pit. Only her grip on my T-shirt held me back from the abyss.

"Pandora Atlas!" she roared. "Give us the clue!"

My T-shirt tore, and I leaned even further over the pit. My feet struggled to get a grip, and I windmilled my arms, as if that might stop me falling. Pan fought as best she could, but she couldn't overpower the mercenaries, who pinned her to the ground.

The goon's grip tightened on my shirt. "Tell us!" she demanded. "Or Jake dies."

"Pan, don't!" I yelled.

My legs were shaking so hard that I could have caused myself to fall. I was trying to act tough, to call her bluff. I still thought she'd pull me back.

Then she let go with one hand.

I slipped even further; she held me at arm's length over the pit. I tried to grab her wrist, but she swatted my hand away. The spider tattoo wriggled as muscles strained in her neck. She was going to let go. They still had Pan, and only Pan knew the clue. I was useless to them...

One of my feet slipped from the ledge and dangled over the pit.

"OK!" Pan called. "I'll tell you!"

"Speak!" the mercenary barked.

Pan's mouth cracked open and the words croaked out.

"It's... It's somewhere on—"

My other foot slipped and my legs slid into the pit. I thought the mercenary had pushed me, but the goon looked just as surprised as me. Now the whole ground jolted and she fell to her knees, just managing to keep hold as I hung in the pit. Was it still collapsing? My feet scrabbled at the rock as the mercenary lifted me up. I gasped thank yous to the woman who had been just about to kill me.

The whole crater was shaking now.

"An earthquake!" one of the goons yelled.

"Look out!" another warned.

They dived to one side as a rock tumbled down the slope, missing us by metres. Another came from the other side, then another – basketball-sized boulders rolling down the crater. One of them hit a mercenary, who flipped up like a skittle and crashed back to the slope.

I scrambled over to Pan, and we helped each other stand.

"What's happening?" she wheezed. "This can't be an earthquake. It's not—"

The crater jolted again, and we tumbled down. Hot air rushed up, followed by a burst of boiling water and steam. Mercenaries collapsed, clutching their faces as if the contents of a kettle had been thrown in their eyes.

Higher up the crater, another geyser burst from between rocks. The air was now thick with steam.

"Pan," I cried, "you said this volcano was extinct!"

"It is!"

"Well, it's come back to life!"

# 22

Pan kept shaking her head as she stared at the chaos all around us. "Jake," she insisted, "this volcano is not active."

"Are you crazy?" I cried. "Look!"

At the top of the crater, more rocks shot up from the slope like corks popping, forced out by pressure from below. Something spluttered from the ground, dazzlingly bright.

"It's lava!" I yelled.

"It can't be, Jake!"

"Stop saying that! Obviously it is!"

Higher up the slope, the steam grew even thicker. It spread around the crater's rim, like it was deliberately encircling us. It was turning darker too. Was it even steam any more? It looked more like smoke – black smoke.

I remembered the scenes from my dreams;

natural disasters destroying the lost civilization: an earthquake, a tsunami, floodwaters... Had the smoke caused the volcano to come back to life?

More rocks cascaded down the slope, another geyser erupted and the crater shook even harder. The mercenary who had almost killed me roared into her smart-goggles, demanding evacuation, but would help arrive in time?

"We have to get out of here," I called to Pan.

We scrambled up the crater, legs burning from the effort; steam and sweat stung our eyes. The slope was shaking so violently that it was impossible to stay upright, so we resorted to a frantic crawl. I glanced down and saw tumbling rocks fall into the pit.

Then something began to rise *from* the pit. A bubble of black liquid, like an inflating balloon.

It swelled into a small, dark dome and then burst, spraying fiery, orange flecks across the base of the crater. More steam gushed from the hole, along with toxic-looking yellow-green gas. I stood halfway up the slope, staring – mesmerized – as the fumes parted to reveal a pool of lava, bubbling and spitting. The liquid fire began to fill the base of the crater like a blocked drain overflowing. It was rising.

"Pan, go!" I wailed.

She was already climbing as fast as she could. Another geyser erupted in our direction. We screamed and covered our heads as scalding water showered the slope. Higher up, the black smoke grew even thicker, a dark wall trapping us in the crater.

Below, the pool of lava rose higher. I could feel the intensity of its heat prickling my skin and frazzling the hairs on my arms. Our clothes were soaked from the steam. Gases drifting up from the volcano stung my eyes, blurring my vision.

The gases swept away as a helicopter rose above the crater. Further down the slope, the mercenaries gathered together and signalled to the pilot. A wire was lowered from the helicopter, and each mercenary clipped a carabiner on its end to a hook on their belt. Now the helicopter rose, lifting them all from the slope so they dangled together in a group hug.

"They're leaving us to die!" Pan breathed.

"And they have the keys," I added.

Pan started screaming things I can't repeat, when a ball of fire spat from the lava pool like a flaming arrow. It hit the helicopter's tail in a burst of sparks. The helicopter lost control and the mercenaries began to spin on the wire. All they could do was cling on as the helicopter whirled around, fell and crashed into the side of the crater.

The impact threw the pilot from the cockpit, but the mercenaries remained connected. The helicopter dragged them with it as it slid tail-first down the slope, towards the lava pool. Some of the goons dug their heels into the surface, as if they might stop the helicopter's slide. Others fumbled with the wire, frantic to get free.

The helicopter's tail slid into the rising lava. The metal twisted and groaned as the fiery monster devoured its prey.

"They're going to die," I gasped.

Pan yanked my arm, urging me further up the slope. "We can't help them. Come on!"

I didn't move. The mercenaries were lost to the horror of their situation. They needed help.

"Jake," Pan called, "are you really going to risk your life for the people who just tried to kill us?"

"Keep going," I replied. "I'll catch up."

"I'm not leaving you! *That's* why I'm coming, not for *them*."

I didn't want her to come, didn't want her to die for my dumb decisions, but I knew she would. In the circumstances, I think it was OK for us to swear a lot as we scrambled around the crater and down to the struggling mercenaries. One of them saw us coming and raised his stun gun.

"Are you crazy?" Pan wailed. "We're trying to save you!"

They slid another few feet down the slope as the helicopter sank deeper into the bubbling lava pool. The gadget connecting them to the wire had twisted, so the mercenaries couldn't unclip themselves.

"Can you shoot it with a stun gun?" Pan asked, as we scrambled closer.

"It's titanium," one of the mercenaries grunted. "It's made *not* to break."

The mercenary who'd almost thrown me into the pit grabbed my arm and yanked me close. "The keys," she snarled.

"I'm not trying to take them," I protested.

"No," she snapped, "you don't understand! Where are they?"

Oh, God. I wiped dirt from my eyes and scanned the slope for my backpack. When I spotted it I almost wished I hadn't. The bag had tumbled down the slope and into the helicopter's open cockpit. One of its straps had caught on a control lever, so it swung in the air as the helicopter shuddered, sinking deeper...

Time froze.

I was aware of the mercenaries and Pan shouting, but it faded into background noise. My eyes moved from the backpack to the mercenaries and along the wire to its winch in the helicopter.

The wire tugged the mercenaries another few feet towards their deaths.

"Is the winch titanium too?" I demanded.

"No, it's steel," one of the mercenaries replied. His voice rose with fresh hope. "Shoot it off and get us free!"

"Jake!" Pan protested. "You are *not* going to that helicopter."

Ignoring my sister, I took a stun gun from the mercenary, and slung the strap over my shoulder.

"It's personally calibrated," she grunted.

"What?" I asked.

"Only I can make it work," she explained. "I've charged it, so it's ready for one shot. That's all you'll have, so get it right."

Pan grabbed my arm so hard I winced. "Jake, did you hear me?"

I did, but what choice did I have? We couldn't just watch these people die – and we'd lose the keys too.

"Pull me up when I grab the line!" I shouted.

Gripping the wire, I shuffled on my backside down the crater, inching towards what was left of the helicopter. One of my feet slipped, but I grasped the wire tighter to stop myself from sliding into the lava.

Sweat poured down my face. The lava radiated such intense heat that I felt my skin blister. Steam clouded the air and volcanic gases stung my eyes. I almost turned and climbed back up, but the mercenaries yelled at me to hurry, and I forced myself to carry on.

The helicopter slid deeper into the molten rock. Parts that weren't even touching the lava began to warp and glow fierce red. I tried not to think of my body melting, skin roasting, bones burning...

I pulled what was left of my T-shirt over my mouth and nose, trying not to breathe the gases. They were making me dizzy. Between the fumes, the steam, the sweat and my stinging eyes, I could barely even see my backpack inside the helicopter. I fumbled to the cockpit, reached to hold onto the metal frame and snatched my hand back with a wail. The metal was scorching. How was I going to get inside? Could I get back out?

The cockpit swayed one way and then the other as the rear of the helicopter slid another few feet into the lava. Two of the rotors dipped into the molten pool and melted like butter. Patches of lava turned silvery grey as it cooled, before dazzling magma oozed out from underneath. The glow was so intense that I had to shield my eyes.

"Jake," Pan hollered, "move!"

I untied the laces on my trainers and reached one foot over the cockpit frame and onto the pilot's seat. My shoe sank into the leather, which had begun to melt. I pulled it free and stepped onto the steel partition behind the cockpit.

I needed to stay calm, but my legs were shaking and the soles of my trainers were melting on the metal. Ignoring them, I reached across the cockpit and unhooked my rucksack from the control lever.

Slowly, I slipped my arm through one of the straps so the bag hung on my shoulder. I pulled the stun gun from my other shoulder and gripped the weapon with quivering hands.

The cockpit shuddered.

I grabbed one of the controls to steady myself and screamed. It was like gripping a hot poker. Searing agony shot up my arm, and I dropped the stun gun. The skin on my hand bubbled and started to blister, making my palm look like a slice of pizza. I clamped it between my legs and wailed.

"Get out of there!" Pan yelled.

One side of the partition I was standing on crumpled and melted. Glowing lava rose through the hole, so bright it was like looking into the sun. It was inches away, and rising higher. With one hand, I grabbed the stun gun and fired at the winch. Sparks ricocheted around the cabin, and more lava spat through the partition. My boots were melted to the metal, but I'd remembered to untie their laces, so I could pull my feet free. I took a socks-only step onto a melting seat, and leaped for the wire outside the cockpit.

The moment I grabbed hold, Pan and the mercenaries pulled the line, hauling it up the slope. It was all I could do to cling on with one hand. Below, the helicopter cockpit sank into the lava with a sickening belch as the volcano devoured its meal.

The mercenaries dragged me closer, and one of them tore the backpack from my shoulder. Pan saw the burns on my hand, my blistered and peeling skin and the welts on my feet. I thought she might hug me. Instead she yelled.

"Get up, we have to move!"

I tried, but something was wrong. I could barely lift myself from the slope, and when I did my legs buckled. The lava was rising faster, bubbling and spluttering. It spat a fire ball that landed a few metres away.

Pan saw me on the ground and slid back down. "What's wrong?" she cried.

"I ... can't move..."

It wasn't my injuries. It was my head. Everything was spinning, like I'd been drugged.

"It's the gas," one of the mercenaries yelled. "He's breathed too much in."

The mercenary scrambled down to help. I was vaguely aware that it was the woman who had tried to throw me into the pit. She lifted one of my eyelids and looked at my pupils.

"We'll carry him," she said. She yelled to her comrades, who had begun to scramble higher up the slope. "Get back here!"

None of them stopped. One of them actually laughed.

"That's Jake Atlas," the goon said.

"This boy just saved your lives!" the female mercenary bellowed.

Most kept climbing, but two of them came back down to help. I wish I could tell you more, but the gas had messed with my head. They picked me up and carried me, which was impressive considering that the crater was shaking, rocks were tumbling, geysers spraying and the lava was rising faster than ever. I felt its heat and saw fireballs explode against the slope. I heard Pan urging the mercenaries to move faster, but I didn't understand much else until I realized I was in the air.

I was rising from the mountain, over the lava-filled crater, attached to a wire. Above me hovered the hulking shape of a helicopter. The mercenaries were fixed to the wire too. I prayed my sister was as well, but I couldn't be sure.

Then, below, I glimpsed something else. The black smoke had risen from the top of the crater and spread across the surface of the lava pool. I was dazed, barely conscious, but I swear I saw a face in that smoke. It wasn't human, and it wasn't animal. It was something ... else. The molten rock beneath it caused its eyes to burn like bonfires, and it was grinning. Somehow I knew – it was grinning at me.

And then, nothing.

# 23

The dream again. This time I only saw the door. The emerald door with the four crystal keys pulsing like hearts.

I stood facing it, aware of the smoke drifting behind me, and that close by an entire civilization was being wiped out. But that door was all that mattered. I sensed it wanted me to move towards it, so I did.

One of the keys glowed brighter. Its crystal dials began to turn; I heard the clockwork clicks even above the chaos of crashing rocks.

*Click, click, click.*

*Click, click.*

"Jake Atlas," a voice said.

The voice was soft, almost a whisper in my ear. It came from behind me.

It was the smoke.

"Jake Atlas. You have been chosen."

I woke, staring at a metal ceiling. I was lying on my back in a bed. In a panic, I remembered the volcano and the helicopter, and I bolted up.

I tried to talk, but all that came out was a rasp. My mouth was so dry I could barely part my lips. Pan held a straw to my mouth, and I sipped water.

"Pan," I gasped, "what's going on?"

"It's OK," Pan said. "We're safe."

She leaned closer and lowered me back onto the bed. Her face was covered in scratches, and a storm of bruises raged down the side of her face. Weirdly, we both wore the same black military suit as the People of the Snake's mercenaries – the uniform of our enemy. My feet had been expertly bandaged and my burned hand rested off the bed, inside a glass case about the size of a shoebox. Both sides of the case were connected to wires and tubes, while a tiny machine inside whirred silently over my palm, like a 3D printer. It tickled, but there was no pain.

Pan nodded towards the glass box. "It's repairing your nerves. And giving you new skin."

I'd guessed that much – but that wasn't my question. "Where are we?"

"We're in a plane, Jake," she said.

I'd guessed that too. The bed I lay on was gyroscopic, so it didn't move even when the plane did, but I could still feel a slight vibration from the plane's powerful engines. Over Pan's shoulder I glimpsed mercenaries at a holosphere the size of a banquet table. They were studying projections of pottery shards, scrolls and 3D plans of archaeological sites. Stun guns and other kit hung in racks on the walls. I could just see the pilot in the cockpit and, through the windscreen, a cloudy night sky.

"Are we caught?" I asked.

Someone behind Pan spoke in a posh voice. "That depends on you."

"Oh, no," I moaned, lying back, "not him again."

Lord Osthwait limped closer, clearing his throat as if I might not have noticed him and he really wanted me to. He'd finally taken off his massive fur coat to reveal a three-piece tweed suit with a little handkerchief in its breast pocket. He looked like a time traveller from another age. I wished he'd naff off back to it.

"Master Atlas," he said, "it would appear that you owe us your life."

A dull ache pounded at the back of my head. I winced and drank more water. The machine healing my hand whirred faster.

"That's funny coming from someone who has tried to kill us several times," I replied.

He brushed an imaginary speck of dust from his sleeve. "Well, then," he said. "Perhaps we are even, and we might consider working together."

Pan looked at me and we both burst out laughing. The twirled ends of Osthwait's moustache rose as his mouth puckered into an outraged sneer. He banged his cane on the floor like a teacher demanding his pupils' attention.

"Would you care to share the joke?" he demanded.

I wiped my eyes, refreshed by the laughter. "Sorry, it's just the idea of teaming up with you lot."

"What do you mean?"

"You've tried to kill us, like, four times."

"Five, I think," Pan added. "If you count the drone attack in Tibet."

Lord Osthwait snorted. "You were trying to sabotage our operation."

"We were trying to uncover the truth," Pan corrected. "A disaster wiped out a whole civilization. You want to cover it up. That makes us the good guys."

Now it was Osthwait who laughed, although it didn't sound like it came naturally to him. "Good guys, bad guys. You regard the world like children."

"Um, we are children."

"No. You sacrificed that right the day you became involved in our operation."

I noticed Pan's scowl soften, and wondered if she was thinking the same thing. Despite everything, the People of the Snake had never treated us like kids. In fact they'd shown us respect, which is a strange thing to say about an organization that tried to kill us four times. Sorry, *five.*

"Our parents," I demanded. "How do we get them back?"

Lord Osthwait nodded thoughtfully, as if the

question concerned him as much as us. "We are not certain," he said.

"Then you're not much use to us," Pan snapped, "because that's all we want to know. So why should we work with you? Only *we* know the location of the fourth key."

"And you have been clever to withhold that information, other than to provide our pilot with a vague direction to travel in," Osthwait admitted.

I glanced at Pan. Even *I* didn't yet know the clue she'd found in the volcano pit.

"I just told them to fly north," she whispered.

"However," Lord Osthwait noted, "with our resources, it would not be impossible to locate the fourth key based solely on that information, and to discard you from our plans. So the question should be why should *we* work with *you*? And there is an answer."

The machine repairing my hand beeped and stopped whirring. One of the mercenaries came over – the woman from the volcano. I'd only met her once, but in that short time she had almost killed me, and then saved my life twice. The spider tattoo seemed to scuttle out from under her collar as she opened the glass box and lifted my hand out. The skin on my palm was totally healed and I could wiggle my fingers without any pain. It was incredible, but I tried not to look impressed.

She smiled, packing up the medical kit. "Good as new," she said.

"Uh, yeah," I muttered. "I mean, thanks."

"You're welcome. My name's Jessica, by the way."

"Oh. OK..."

It was a bit awkward for a few seconds, neither of us knowing what to say. Should we keep arguing? That felt like the natural thing to do, but maybe Osthwait was right. The Roman guard told us that we had to defeat the smoke to free our parents from its realm, whatever that meant. Maybe working with the People of the Snake was our best chance to do that. They knew more than us about what was going on, after all.

"The black smoke," Pan asked, "what is it?"

"Please, Miss Atlas," Osthwait replied. "You know perfectly well what it is."

Pan's grip tightened on the side of my bed.

"Pan?" I said. "What does he mean?"

"I mean your sister is fully aware of the true nature of the power you call the black smoke. It would be impossible for someone of such superior intellect not to have formed an opinion on the matter, and, being of superior intellect, she would be confident that her opinion is correct."

"Pan? What's he talking about?"

"Jake," Pan said, "the smoke sent us through time, and from one place to another. It can cause earthquakes, volcanoes..."

"But what is it, Pan?"

"It's... It's a god."

*"What?"*

"Not a god," Lord Osthwait corrected. "It is *the* god.

The first civilization worshipped it, but they also feared it. The god was vicious, vengeful and vain. It demanded sacrifices in its name. If it wasn't honoured highly enough, it wrought death and destruction upon the civilization. Eventually the people turned against it. They devised a plan to remove the god from their lives, by trapping it."

"Behind the door," I muttered. "The emerald door..."

I don't know why I said that – I was just thinking aloud, trying to piece it all together. The mercenary stopped packing up the medical kit and looked at me with one eyebrow cocked.

"Door?" she said.

"How intriguing," Osthwait added. "Did you have some sort of dream, Jake? Or perhaps a vision? Has the god chosen *you*?"

"What do you mean, chosen him?" Pan asked.

"The civilization failed to trap the god entirely," Lord Osthwait explained. "Part of it – a fraction – remained in our world."

"A fraction?"

"That *fraction* had caused earthquakes, volcanoes... The thought of what the whole thing could do made me feel dizzy, and I wanted to lie down again.

"It wishes to become fully free," Osthwait continued, but it needs assistance. I wonder if it has chosen young Jake as its helper."

I laughed, although I didn't find what he said at all funny. "That's a load of rubbish," I insisted. "I don't even know what I saw. Some sort of door, that's all."

"Not just any door," Osthwait said. "A very significant door. The portal through which the god passed between its world and ours. But the lost civilization built four keys, which when used together would stop the god from passing through. When it discovered their betrayal, the god grew furious, causing earthquakes, volcanos and immense tsunamis. The civilization succeeded in trapping all but part of the god, but at a cost. It destroyed them and their homeland, which sank beneath the sea. Only a fragment of this land remained."

"You mean, as an island?" Pan asked.

"Perhaps," Osthwait agreed. "All we know is that this was where Marcus Turbo found the door. The god had spared that fragment because it wanted the door to be found. It wanted to be free again."

"But why were there only three keys in the door when Turbo found it?"

Lord Osthwait's mouth puckered with a mix of surprise and annoyance, as if I'd just asked the most stupidly obvious question in the history of stupidly obvious questions.

"As their world was destroyed, the few survivors of the lost civilization took the one of the keys, without which the other three would never work. They hid it in a sacred mountain in Tibet. They left markers in tombs around the world – emerald tablets documenting their story. Of course you know this tale."

*All too well*, I thought. A year ago, we had begun this

hunt by searching for those emerald tablets, which were buried with the survivors of the lost civilization.

"So why did the Romans take the keys from the door?" Pan asked.

Osthwait nodded to Jessica, giving her permission to answer.

Jessica came forward and spoke. I sensed she was second-in-command around here.

"We believe the Praetorians were on a mission to scout new land," she explained. "They were searching for riches – gold or jewels. The Romans only conquered lands they felt would be worth the effort."

"So the Praetorians found the door," Pan said. "It had the three keys in it, which they took as proof of riches beyond the empire."

"But in doing so," Lord Osthwait added, "one of the keys was disturbed. Its cogs were moved. You know the result."

"The black smoke," I muttered. "That's the 'fragment' of the god that stayed in this world."

"Indeed," Osthwait confirmed. "Moving the cogs seems to summon it, which the Romans discovered the hard way."

I remembered the cult chamber mural of Marcus Turbo's troops battling the swirling black cloud...

"Fraction?"

"Marcus Turbo knew that he had made a mistake," Osthwait continued. "The Praetorians had encountered a force that was not of this world. Something to be respected, worshipped and feared. That cohort of soldiers formed a secret society, a cult dedicated to worshipping the power while also ensuring it could never harm Rome. They believed the keys had to be separated and kept as far from Rome as possible."

"They were right," Pan said. "Surely we should keep them apart, or destroy them or something."

"No," Osthwait disagreed. "We need to return the keys to the door. All of them. Then we can trap it securely behind the door before... Well, before it escapes and brings about the apocalypse."

"Apocalypse?" Pan asked. "Do you really think it would destroy the world?"

"Let me put it this way, Miss Atlas. If you were imprisoned by ants for ten thousand years, once you escaped would you not crush the anthill?"

"I like ants."

"Well, this god does not like humans. Destroying us would be its pleasure, and just as simple as crushing an anthill would be to you."

"Hang on," I said. "The door. Where is it?"

"It's a treasure hunt, Master Atlas. We have to find the clues. But we have come this far. I believe we can play this game to its end. Not, however, without the final key."

Weirdly, I believed Lord Osthwait. The fact was, we'd stand a far better chance of success with them on our side. If nothing else, they could get us wherever it was we needed to go.

"Give us back the keys and we'll give you the clue," I demanded.

Lord Osthwait cleared his throat and glanced at Pan, who shrugged and nodded towards the floor. My backpack sat by her feet. It was half open, and I could see the keys inside.

"He gave them back already," she muttered.

"As a sign of trust," Osthwait added.

Pan and I looked at each other, exchanging eye signals and then shrugs, a silent conversation like our parents often had. Finally she sighed and told Osthwait what she knew.

"Before the pit collapsed," she said, "I read a clue."

"*Vallum Aelium*," Lord Osthwait replied.

"Wait," Pan gasped. "You already knew?"

"An educated guess," the lord explained. "An extremely educated one."

"Hang on," I protested. "*Vallum Aelium?* I've never heard of it."

"Yes, you have," Pan said. "Although that's its Roman title."

"So what's its non-Roman title?"

"Hadrian's Wall."

She was right: even *I* had heard of that. "You mean *the* Hadrian's Wall?"

"Yeah, that one. We know that the Praetorians took the keys beyond the borders of their empire. Hadrian's Wall was one of those borders."

"OK, but isn't that, like, a thousand miles long?"

"Sixty-nine miles," Osthwait corrected. "And we have three hours before we arrive in England to solve where exactly along its length Marcus Turbo took the key."

"So how do we do that?" I asked.

"The old-fashioned way." He prodded the end of his cane towards the holosphere table. "We study."

I groaned – that wasn't my idea of the old-fashioned way. I noticed Pan's eyes light up with excitement. This mission was now in her territory. As I watched Osthwait and Jessica follow my sister to the holosphere, I felt a little out of place. Everyone on this plane seemed to have a job other than me. And there was still one thing I didn't understand...

"Wait," I called. "How do you know so much?"

"I beg your pardon?" Lord Osthwait asked.

"You knew about Marcus Turbo, and the Praetorians, and about the lost civilization, their tombs and the keys. How?"

Lord Osthwait's mouth curled a little at the edges, into something like a smile. I think he'd just realized that, actually, there was an even more stupid and more obvious question that could be asked, and I just had, and it amused him.

"Well, it is our history," he replied.

"I... Your history?"

"Of course. Marcus Turbo is the founder of this organization. The secret society he created – it is us."

# 24

The plane window trembled as I pressed my head against the glass, gazing at the dawn-lit land below. A sheen of mist hung over patchwork fields and narrow country lanes enclosed by hedgerows.

England.

Home.

According to my goggles, the area we were flying over wasn't far from where we used to live. Our comfy home, identical to all the others in its suburban estate: my bedroom full of clutter and comics, and Pan's, with its walls plastered with heavy metal band posters. Along the corridor was Mum and Dad's room, with huge sliding-door cupboards in which every item of clothing was folded like it was on sale in a fancy shop. A door from their bedroom led to a study, where they'd spent so many evenings marking college papers. I wondered how much of that time they'd been thinking about their old lives, before they'd given up treasure hunting and settled down in the suburbs.

Back then, Mum had always seemed so agitated, I guess because her whole life was uncomfortable. No matter how she tried to wear it, it didn't fit. She claimed she and Dad had come out of retirement because of all the antiquities being destroyed by the People of the Snake, but I knew the real reason. They missed it. The thrill, the adventure, the danger. This past year was the only time I'd ever seen them really happy. There had been a glint in their eyes, even in the most dangerous moments. *Especially* in those moments. They had been themselves.

That, more than anything, boiled my blood.

They knew how it felt to lose this life, and yet they had made us promise to do the same.

We could still walk away. We could give the People of the Snake the keys and leave them to it. But what if they failed? Pan and I were good at this; they needed our help to save the world. How could we turn our backs on that?

If we did save Mum and Dad, they'd know we broke our promise. But they would be alive.

Pan, Lord Osthwait and the mercenaries were busy at the holosphere table, scanning files and examining holograms of artefacts. Pan spotted something on one and enlarged an area to show Osthwait, causing the lord's bushy eyebrows to rise in surprise. Pan was running the show, beaming with excitement.

Not many things made Pan feel that way. Mum and Dad should never take this from her.

I looked down again at the mist-shrouded countryside. It didn't feel right to call it "home". I shifted in my seat, gazing around the plane, and then at the backpack at my feet that contained the keys.

Really, this world was my home.

I was never going back.

Jessica approached, offering a plate with a sandwich and some crisps. She looked wary, as if I might slap it from her hand, which – in truth – I actually considered doing.

"Must be a while since you ate," she said, edging closer.

I didn't know what to say. Accepting anything from these guys felt wrong, but it was a tuna melt – my favourite sandwich – and I was starving. I took the plate, trying not to look too grateful.

"Thanks," I mumbled. "But we don't owe you goons anything."

"Can you stop calling us that?" Jessica replied.

"Eh?"

"Goons. It's offensive. We're trained soldiers. I worked for eleven years in military intelligence, but you talk to us like we're henchmen to Bond villains."

I looked away and muttered, "Whatever."

She came up beside me and peered through the window.

"Does it feel strange?" she asked. "To be home?"

I just shrugged, eager not to give anything away, and devoured the sandwich.

"I've not really thought about it," I said between bites.

She smiled – she actually looked friendly – and sat next to me on the bench. The plane shuddered as we passed through turbulence, and she gripped the side of the seat.

"I don't like flying much," she said.

I gave a snort that I hoped said, "That's weird, but I don't want to acknowledge it."

"What?" she asked.

"Well, they fly you all over the world."

"I have had to travel a lot, yes. It's not easy. I have two children."

I shifted on the bench, but really I was uncomfortable with the conversation. These mercenaries had always been faceless enemies, and that suited me fine. I'm not sure I liked hearing about their lives. But at the same time I was intrigued.

"Do they know their mum works for an evil organization?" I asked.

"No, because I don't. I work for an organization that is trying to save the world. I just assure them that I am safe."

"So you lie to them?"

"Yes, like you lied to your parents."

I almost choked. Was she guessing, or did she really know? I swallowed hard, trying not to give anything away, but she smiled and handed me a glass of water.

"I don't think you realize the scale of our operation to track your family," she continued. "Thousands of operatives, control centres in twelve countries. At times I wondered whether our mission was to find the keys or to find you. There was barely a moment in the past few months that you were not under surveillance."

It made sense, thinking how the People of the Snake had tracked us in Kathmandu, and how quickly they'd appeared at the museum in Rome. They'd let us lead them to the keys.

"It's not cool to gloat," I muttered.

"I'm not."

"Then why are you telling me?"

"So you know that I understand why you're here."

"We're saving the world, aren't we?"

"No, you're here because this is where, deep down, you *want* to be. Do you know why we directed such resources into following you? Because you're the best. You're a natural treasure hunter; it's in your blood. None of us wants to be your enemy. Jake, if we succeed that won't be the end of this mission."

"What do you mean?"

"I mean there are more elements than just this battle."

"What elements?"

"*Complicated* elements, for which we would love your help, and Pan's. As extremely skilled operatives, you would work for us at the highest level and be rewarded appropriately."

"We don't need your money."

"But you'd receive it anyway, which can't hurt."

I shook my head and looked away, watching Pan working with Lord Osthwait and the mercenaries at the holosphere. There was no way we'd ever take money from these guys; that was never why my family did this. But increasingly I was realizing that the People of the Snake weren't really our enemies; they just had a rubbish way of going about things.

"Let me ask you," Jessica continued, "which of all those people at that holosphere do you think will uncover our next clue?"

"Pan, obviously."

"Now imagine if she wasn't here. If you had kept your promise to your parents, what then?"

As if on cue, Pan did a little skip and clapped her hands. She'd found something, but I was surprised to see her high-five a couple of the mercenaries around the holosphere. She even gave Lord Osthwait a quick fist bump.

"Jake," she called. "Come check this out."

Jessica had just proved a point, so I avoided looking at her as I rushed to join my sister. Pan had created a virtual museum: dozens of hologram artefacts hovered over the glass surface. Most of them were identical – square scraps of wood covered in spidery black writing. Only one was different, and even less impressive: a tiny scrap of a scroll. It was the sort of display I'd walk right past in an actual museum, but whatever this stuff was, it had Pan so excited she had to take a sip of water before she could speak.

With two fingers she pinched the hologram of the scroll, enlarging its faded Latin lines. "Jake, this is a fragment of a document from Eboracum."

"OK, you know I don't know where that is."

Lord Osthwait cleared his throat, indicating that it was his turn to speak. One of his mercenaries had prepared tea for him, which he drank from a delicate china cup and saucer. It looked out of place among all that military technology.

"Eboracum is the Roman name for the city of York," he explained. "We searched for references to Marcus Turbo and Praetorian Guards anywhere near Hadrian's Wall around the time we believe they travelled there. Your sister found this scroll, documenting a meeting between Praetorians and the leaders of a Roman legion at Eboracum."

"Jake," Pan added breathlessly, "that legion was the Ninth."

She gave another excited clap, as if she'd just witnessed the final flourish of a magic trick. It was obviously supposed to mean something to me, but I just blinked.

"Jake," Pan continued, "the story of the Ninth Legion is one of the most famous in ancient history."

"Well, I'm not going to suddenly remember it," I said.

"Indeed," Lord Osthwait muttered. "The Ninth

Legion was the finest fighting unit in the Roman army. Sometime after the year 122, they vanished."

"Vanished?"

"Five thousand soldiers," Pan said, "disappeared from all records. That was almost exactly the time we think the Praetorians came here, and when Marcus Turbo disappeared too."

I rubbed my eyes. My head was still woozy from the volcanic gas, and I was struggling to keep up. "So you think Turbo and his Praetorians recruited the Ninth Legion?" I asked.

"Well," Pan replied, "all this document proved was that they met. But then we found this..."

She flicked away the scroll hologram, dismissive of the document that only a minute ago she'd gazed at like a holy relic. Instead she brought forward one of the wooden squares so that it hovered over the glass at eye level.

"This is one of the Vindolanda tablets," she announced.

"I can't imagine that means much to Jake either," Lord Osthwait said.

I expected Pan to swear at him, but she was too excited by her discovery to notice his swipe. "They're a hoard of letters written on wooden tablets by Roman soldiers guarding a fort on Hadrian's Wall called Vindolanda," she explained. "They were written around the time we think Turbo arrived with the key. In this particular letter, written in the year 134, a soldier at the fort grumbles about having to unload huge amounts of supplies: food, ale, hay for horses, stuff like that."

"So?" I asked.

"Those are far more supplies than they needed at the fort, Jake. Enough, in fact, to support a whole legion setting off on an expedition. And Vindolanda is the logical fort on the Wall to travel to from Eboracum. One road connected the two places."

She was talking so fast that I was starting to feel dizzy. "Wait, let me get this straight," I said. So Marcus Turbo and the Praetorians recruited the Ninth Legion at Eboracum and then marched with them to this fort, Vindowhatever."

"Vindolanda," Lord Osthwait corrected. "Where this evidence suggests they prepared for a major expedition in the year 134. It is possible that expedition departed to carry the key north of the Wall, beyond the edge of the empire. Shortly after that, they all vanished: Turbo, the Praetorians, the Legion and the keys."

"So what happened to them?" I asked.

The plane shuddered, and I realized that we had begun our descent to land. Pan grinned, a huge sparkling smile. She clapped her hands so hard that all of the holograms flickered.

"That's what we're going to find out," she said.

# 25

If you like cream teas, then I highly recommend the visitor centre tea room at Vindolanda Fort on Hadrian's Wall. They'd run out of clotted cream when we turned up, but Betty, the tea lady, bakes the best scones I've ever tasted. It's worth the trip just to try them – they may be the most exciting thing about the whole place.

Two thousand years ago, Hadrian's Wall dominated the northern English countryside, a ten-foot high stone barrier defended by eighty towers and seventeen forts. Vindolanda was one of the largest forts. It was home to hundreds of soldiers whose main job was to look scary to any enemy tribes that thought about causing trouble. In Roman times the Wall really *looked* Roman – a stern symbol of power. Locals had never seen anything like it.

Today, it looks much more English. Its crumbled

remains dip and rise along gentle hills speckled with sheep or purpled with spongy heather. Children on school trips scramble up and over it without breaking into a sweat, and in the summer its once imposing towers become nesting grounds for visiting swallows. The Romans built the Wall to roar "Don't mess with us!", but today it whispers "No drama here, everything is fine."

It's hard to imagine Vindolanda Fort as anything other than a neatly arranged pile of rubble. The archaeological site spills across a green valley, reached by a country road with an old pub called The Sheep and Cloth Cap or The Cow and Wellington Boot or something like that. (I never actually saw its name; the building was destroyed shortly after we arrived by a massive tower of... Well, I'll get to that.) Everything at the site is labelled with information plaques, and the lawns between the ruins are mowed in perfect pinstripes.

Then there's the visitor centre, which is by far the most English thing about the whole place. The squat brick building has only three rooms: Betty's tea room, a small office for the site manager, and a museum boasting a papier-mâché recreation of the fort, a few information boards and an old TV showing a 1990s documentary about the soldiers that lived there. My mum would have loved every bit of it. It was a quiet, safe, pleasant place.

But not for much longer.

We had landed at a military base fifty miles south of the fort. Lord Osthwait presented papers that sent the soldiers into a total panic, rushing to gather vehicles, food, maps and various bits of kit we'd need for our mission to the Wall. The base sergeant got into a flap trying to impress Osthwait, snapping his heels together and saluting each time either of them finished a sentence. It was hard not to be impressed by the effect of the organization's arrival. I knew they controlled police forces around the world, but bossing a whole army about was something else.

That's what made turning up at Vindolanda so funny. I've never seen anyone so unimpressed by the People of the Snake as Betty, the tea lady. She emerged from the visitor centre staring at us as if aliens had arrived from another galaxy – not surprised to see aliens, just baffled as to why they'd come *here.* She brushed flour from her apron, and called out, "Visitors' car park is round the back."

Lord Osthwait approached, leaning on his cane and doing his best impression of a smile. "Madam," he replied, "we are not visitors."

She looked even less impressed. "Well, the car park is actually for everyone."

Osthwait's grip tightened on the top of his cane. He was more used to the reception we'd received at the military base. "No, madam, we are here on important business."

"Clotted cream?"

"I beg your pardon?"

"Are you from the farm? We're out of clotted cream."

"I… Perhaps I could speak with the site manager."

"You can, once you've parked."

I watched with Pan from the Jeep, delighted to see Lord Osthwait struggle.

"I like this lady already," Pan whispered.

After we'd parked, Betty insisted Osthwait bought tickets for himself and each of his mercenaries, although she offered a group discount. When the site manager, Dr Naunton, finally appeared from his office, his shirt was crumpled, and a line of drool was hanging in his thick, brown beard. He'd obviously been napping, but was wide awake the moment Osthwait presented him with a file of official papers.

"You are in control of this site?" Osthwait asked.

Dr Naunton managed a small nod.

"Not any more," Osthwait continued. "This document, ratified by a treaty between thirty-two countries, hands me control."

Dr Naunton stared past us to the mercenaries unloading kit from the Jeeps, then he gazed around his quiet little visitor centre. He was so flabbergasted that his mind went into academic autopilot, focusing on the only part of Osthwait's statement it could challenge.

"Which thirty-two countries?"

"I beg your pardon?" Osthwait asked.

"Is the UK one of them?"

Ha! I'd never seen Osthwait look so thrown. He blinked several times, grunted and muttered something, then stared at his papers. The answer obviously wasn't there. "Well, I would assume so..." he mumbled. "Sir, we have travelled a considerable distance on urgent international business associated with the preservation of life on this planet. We could take this site by force if we desire."

"Sounds like you all need a cup of tea," Betty said.

"I'd love a scone," I called.

Betty headed back to the kitchen. "I'll bake a fresh batch. But we've no clotted cream, I'm afraid. I hoped you were the farmer."

Betty insisted we *all* had a cream tea. Lord Osthwait wasn't pleased, but I didn't see any mercenaries complaining as they topped up their mugs and piled jam on their scones. Pan and I scoffed three scones each, and Jessica joined us too.

Dr Naunton brushed scone crumbs from his beard, and finally asked what he'd been scared to ask until now. "So *why* are you here?"

Lord Osthwait picked up his tea and sipped it slowly for dramatic effect. "We can only reveal a small amount of our business," he replied.

"We're searching for the missing Ninth Legion," I said. "We think they marched from here with a Roman soldier superstar named Marcus Turbo, carrying one of four keys that we need to save the world from a really annoyed god."

"And … that's a *small* amount of your business?" Dr Naunton replied.

Lord Osthwait sighed and set down his tea. "No, that is everything."

Dr Naunton stared at each of us, searching for any trace of a smile to suggest this was a joke. Finding none, he scratched his beard as he tried to process what I'd just blurted out. Most of it probably seemed like what my mum would call mumbo jumbo, crack-pot conspiracy rubbish. But one detail had grabbed his interest as a historian.

"There's no evidence of the Ninth Legion at this fort," he said.

"One of the Vindolanda tablets from the year 134," Pan explained, "says that—"

"I know what it says," the doctor interrupted. "I excavated those tablets and made the first translation."

He puffed out his chest a little, growing in confidence now that this was an academic debate. "This was a significant fort on the Wall," he continued, "garrisoning around three hundred soldiers. It was isolated, with little quality farming land. Once winter set in, the soldiers here were on their own. It is likely that the tablet to which you refer simply records the arrival of winter supplies."

Pan bit her lip and glanced nervously at Lord Osthwait. She'd not thought about that, but the lord waved the issue away with a flap of his hand.

"Nevertheless," he said, "this is the fort Marcus Turbo would have travelled to from York, so it remains the focus of our investigation. Miss Atlas?"

Pan flinched with surprise. "What?"

"Perhaps you could suggest a plan?"

"I... Oh. OK. Well, we need to suss out where the Romans would have marched. Are there maps of the area north of this fort around the time we think Turbo came here?"

"A few, yes," Dr Naunton replied.

"We will need those," Osthwait demanded.

"Say please," Betty snapped.

Lord Osthwait looked at her as if she'd asked him to balance a jelly on his head.

"Madam, need I remind you of the urgency of our operation?"

"Doesn't mean you can't say please."

"Very well. Please may we requisition your maps?"

"You know, I reckon we could use some extra funding here too, right?" Betty added. "Isn't that so, doc?"

Dr Naunton glanced back and forth between Osthwait and Betty, unsure who he feared the most. "W... Well, this visitor centre is quite old..."

"Fine," Osthwait agreed. "We'll provide a new visitor centre. Now may we continue?"

"I could use a new kettle too," Betty added.

I was loving this. The way Osthwait kept snorting reminded me of the volcano in Morocco spitting molten lava. He was about to explode.

"May I remind everyone," he seethed, "that we are on a mission to save the *world* rather than a tea room?"

"No point in saving the world if you can't find a good tea room," Betty muttered.

# 26

So out from the visitor centre went the papier-mâché fort and most of the tea room's tables. In their place the mercenaries set up their holosphere table, satellite communications and other high-tech stuff. I'm not sure they needed it; it just seemed to be what they did everywhere they went, like a nesting instinct. The rest of us sat in the tea room, examining maps of the region north of Vindolanda in Roman times. Pan, Lord Osthwait and Dr Naunton had some pretty heated squabbles over the route Marcus Turbo would have taken from the Wall. Today, the countryside out there is pleasant. Two thousand years ago, to the Romans, it was deadly. The tribes that lived beyond the Wall *hated* the Roman invaders. Turbo knew the destructive power of the keys; there was no way he'd want one of them to fall into enemy hands.

We were lucky to have Dr Naunton, who knew the

location of every known ancient tribal village, but he was lucky to have us too. Osthwait had access to satellite geophysical reports, echolocation soundscapes and super-high-definition satellite imagery, which together revealed remains of tribal villages that the doctor had no idea had ever existed. Every time they marked a new one on the map he scratched his beard and mumbled about it being impossible, although he clearly believed it.

Eventually they agreed upon the only route that Turbo, the Praetorians and the Ninth Legion could have taken, and superimposed it over a satellite map sixth scone and started paying attention. The map showed about fifty miles of farmland and hills and then a blue stain spreading north for about the same distance – a huge lake surrounded by woodland.

"Kielder Water," Dr Naunton muttered.

"You think the Romans went that way by boat?" Pan asked.

"No, this lake wasn't there in ancient times," Dr Naunton explained. "It was created in the twentieth century when a dam was built. The forest was planted then too."

"What was there before the lake?" I asked.

"A valley, probably bogs and mud. It was tough territory for marching, but it's the only safe route that far. Only..." He cursed under his breath, rubbing his beard again. "No, actually, they can't have gone that way," he said.

"Why not?" Pan asked.

"Because all this region –" on the map, Dr Naunton tapped the area north of the lake and forest – "was occupied by a tribe that the Romans knew were weak. So it makes sense that they would march this way, confident that they could defeat this tribe more than any others."

"So that's good, right?" I asked. "It suggests they went that way."

Dr Naunton shook his head slowly, staring around the map. "No," he said. "You see, this particular tribe was definitely *not* defeated in battle at any time around the date you believe Marcus Turbo was here. They chronicled their history meticulously, every victory and every defeat. None of the documents suggest any interaction with the Romans whatsoever. In fact, they thrived well beyond this time."

"Maybe the Romans made peace with them and the tribe let them pass?" Pan suggested.

"No chance," Dr Naunton replied. "None of these tribes would ever do that."

"How can you be so sure?"

"Twenty years of study."

*Fair enough*, I thought, although Pan huffed a little at the reply. But I didn't understand why they all looked so deflated all of a sudden.

"So what's wrong?" I asked. "You've nailed it."

Dr Naunton looked at me like I was an idiot, then rose from his chair and stretched his back. "We'll try again. There may be another route Turbo could have taken."

"Wait," I protested. "What are you all talking about? We've found the route."

"No, Jake," Pan muttered, a little embarrassed by my continued ignorance, "the Romans can't have marched north of this lake because–"

"I know," I interrupted. "And they can't have gone any other way. So we've cracked it."

Pan sighed, struggling to remain patient. She was about to explain again, when the words caught in her throat and her eyes shot open wide. Finally she understood what I meant.

"Jake, you're right! We *have* nailed it!"

She pulled the map closer, and babbled excitedly. She was grinning now like the Cheshire Cat. I'm not sure I've ever seen her so excited, even when we've found tombs full of treasure. "What Jake means is that if they couldn't go any other way, then they went this way. And if they didn't march north of this lake, then they never *made it* north of this lake. This valley, right here where the lake is now, is where Marcus Turbo, the Praetorian Guards and the whole Ninth Legion vanished forever. This is where we'll find them. This is where we'll find the final key."

# 27

Another thing I'll say about the People of the Snake: once they decided to go somewhere, they didn't waste any time. Mercenaries barked orders and Jeeps were filled with duffel bags of kit and supplies of food and water. It was pretty stressful to watch, but a nice change from how things were done in my family. If Mum and Dad had agreed we needed to reach this forest, they'd have spent a fortnight researching every type of tree in the place before even thinking of going there.

I'd been a bystander for most of the history chat, so it felt good to be on the move.

Pan seemed to have the opposite feeling. She loved all the academic debate, but now that we were off on a mission she looked hesitant, unsure. She watched the mercenaries prepare, chewing the inside of her cheek.

"We're off to find another key," she muttered. "It didn't end well last time."

"Yeah, but this time we've got an army on our side," I replied.

She turned and looked at me. "You're impressed by them, aren't you?"

I shrugged – there was no point in denying it, she knew me too well. "At least we're doing something."

"We were *doing something* before, Jake. We can't trust any of this lot."

I shrugged again. "Jessica isn't so bad. And it's pretty cool, isn't it? Unlimited money, and all that tech."

"We didn't need all that before."

"Pan, we barely did anything before."

"Are you crazy?" A few of the mercenaries looked at us as Pan's voice rose. One of them gave us a military hand signal that I think meant "We're ready to go", and Pan gave one back that meant something ruder.

"Jake, *we* found all the keys," she insisted. "You, me, Mum and Dad, remember?"

"Of course I remember. But imagine if we'd had all of *this* too."

"So you want to replace Mum and Dad with these goons?"

"Don't call them that, it's rude. And, anyway, you seemed pretty friendly with Lord Snooty earlier."

"I was searching for a clue to find our parents. That's all that was, Jake."

She sounded convincing, but that didn't explain

how excited she'd been. Lord Osthwait had let her lead the search. Mum and Dad had never given her that much responsibility.

"Jake, Pan!"

Jessica leaned out of one of the Jeeps. "Why are you standing around?" she called. "Osthwait wants you in here. We're the lead team."

I glanced at Pan, wondering if she'd heard. *Lead team.* If she did, she didn't show it as she followed me to the Jeep. Dr Naunton joined us too, but Lord Osthwait drew the line at Betty coming along, assuring her that we'd all need cream teas on our return.

We drove north from the Wall along country lanes so narrow that the Jeep brushed hedgerow on either side. We'd been to some crazy places recently, compared with which the northern English countryside looked pretty tame. But you'd be a fool to think this world wasn't wild. For starters, you never knew what the English weather would throw at you. The sky had been clear when we'd arrived a few hours ago, but now it was grey and black and swollen with rain. The first drops fell in a drizzle, but the further north we drove, the harder the Jeep's windscreen wipers had to work.

"Are there anoraks among all your fancy kit?" Pan asked.

"Your uniforms are fully waterproof," Jessica replied. She steered the Jeep off the road and along a rutted track that weaved between tall fir trees.

"They're also graphine lined for shock protection, thermally regulated to your specific body temperatures, fireproof, bulletproof and odourproof."

"Cool!" I exclaimed.

"Why odourproof?" Pan asked.

"We've met you a few times, remember," Jessica explained. "We know Jake stinks."

"Hey!" I cried.

Despite her uncertainty, Pan smiled. "You kinda do," she agreed.

"I have something else for you two," Jessica added.

She tapped a spot on the dashboard. Two metal tubes rose from the surface with a cool swishing sound. "Go ahead and take them," she said.

I plucked one of the tubes from its slot, perhaps a little too eagerly, studied it for a few seconds and then pressed one of its ends. The canister split open, revealing a sleek new pair of smart-goggles. They looked like the ones we'd been using, only *way* cooler. They were so light I could barely feel them as I lifted them from their case.

"We call them ultra-goggles," Jessica explained. "They have the usual specifications, infrared, ultrasonic, thermal imaging, periscope view, and a zoom function so powerful you could spot a fly on an ancient ruin from a mile. They also have stun chargers built into the frames, to fire shots from the front or rear, and they can be set to detonate a highly destructive plasma charge."

I was about to put them on, but that last bit of information caused me to reconsider. Jessica noticed and laughed.

"Don't worry, we'll give you training," she explained. "In fact if there's anything at all you guys want to be trained in, just say. We have access to world experts in every skill or subject, so you'd be taught by the best."

"Cool," I repeated.

"Cool?" Pan asked. She'd not even touched the other tube. "Jake, we already have smart-goggles, remember? Same ones as Mum and Dad, and they're fine. And they just happened to have these? Two pairs perfectly sized and calibrated for us, just like they had these outfits?"

A muscle twitched in Jessica's neck, but she smiled. "We're like Cub Scouts," she replied. "Always prepared."

I leaned closer to Pan and whispered. "We may as well use them. Freebies."

"They're weapons, Jake. What's that got to do with archaeology?"

"Pan, we're way past archaeology now."

She stared at me for a moment like she was trying to solve a puzzle. Then she turned and gazed out at the rain-soaked countryside.

"England," she muttered. "So why does this feel like the furthest we've ever been from home?"

# 28

By the time we reached the lake, the rain was hammering on the Jeep roof so hard that we had to shout to be heard. The sky above the trees was ten shades of grey, one of which was basically black. Fir trees creaked as they swayed in the wind, and crows squabbled at their tops, rocking back and forth like sailors in a storm. The trees were packed so tightly that the narrow dirt track we'd taken to reach the lake was the *only* way to reach it. On either side, the forest was dense and dark. It was strange to think it was a new forest; it felt as ancient as any woodland I'd ever known.

You'd never have guessed the lake was new, either. It seemed to stretch forever along a valley through the heart of the forest. The hill on the opposite bank to where we'd stopped was thick with trees right down to the water's edge. On this side, though, a small slope led down to a narrow shore that was a grassy swamp, although the People of the Snake's mercenaries had found a dry enough patch to set up their operations tent. I sheltered inside it with Pan while the mercenaries unloaded kit from the Jeeps and Dr Naunton unrolled his maps of the region in ancient times.

"The lake is forty-four kilometres long," he said. "We'll need boats, and specialists in underwater archaeology. If we divide it into quadrants, we can examine each in sequence and search the entire lakebed over the course of around three months, I'd say."

Lord Osthwait pulled his fur coat tighter, and brushed rain from its sleeve. "Dr Naunton," he replied, "we do not have boats, and we certainly do not have three months."

He nodded to Jessica, signalling for her to wheel over one of the crates that the mercenaries had unloaded. Jessica opened it to reveal a mini submarine, like a silver torpedo, rigged on its underside with tiny cameras and sensors.

"This is a SPURV," she explained, "a special purpose underwater research vehicle, operated remotely from the lake shore."

"SPURV?" I asked. "Isn't there a better name? Can we call it an aquahunter?"

"No," she said. "We have two of them to operate from the shore, both equipped with a plenoptic camera for high-resolution imagery even in low light and murky water, stereo imaging systems to create a composite 3D model of the lakebed and submersible multifrequency magnetic—"

She smiled, seeing the confusion on Dr Naunton's face.

"They're fancy metal detectors," she summarized.

A drop of snot dripped from Dr Naunton's nose. He stared at the machine, baffled by the technology. Pan, though, was totally into it. She edged closer and stroked the device as if it were a beloved pet. She may not have cared about the People of the Snake's military tech, but now we were back to archaeology, she was fascinated.

"How long will they take to search the whole lake?" she asked.

"They can each scan a fifty-metre area of the lakebed at a time, moving at five knots," Osthwait said.

Pan shot him a look, recognizing the challenge. "Eighteen days, then," she fired back.

"Eighteen days?" I replied. "Can't they go faster?"

"We'd risk missing something," Jessica explained. "We can set their sensors to detect the exact material used to make the keys. Five knots is the fastest it can travel at that level of specificity."

Dr Naunton wiped his nose with the sleeve of his anorak. "Hold on," he said. "We're looking for the Ninth Legion too, aren't we? Why not set them to detect Roman armour or weapons?"

"The key is our mission," Osthwait insisted, "and only the key."

"But if we find it," Pan asked, "can we still excavate the site? To find the lost legion?"

Osthwait gave the slightest tilt of his head. "Perhaps *after* we have saved all of humanity from destruction."

Pan grinned, and I sensed then that maybe she really *was* more interested in the archaeology than our mission to save the world. She turned to stare out of the tent and across the rain-battered surface of the lake.

"Then let's get to work," she said.

"Let's get to work" sounds like it should be followed by some serious action. In fact, it took ages for the mercenaries to set up the aquahunters – that's what I'm calling them, OK? – and test that both sent their images to screens in the operations tent. Jessica and I would operate the submarines from the lake shore using mini-tablet computers, so she gave me a lesson, even though I felt sure I could suss it out as we went along. She insisted on teaching me how to use my new smart-goggles, too, which took ages. Pan refused to listen to that part. She hadn't even taken hers from their case.

Osthwait put Pan and Dr Naunton in charge of studying the results in the operations tent. I'd never seen my sister so *into* something. From the moment we lowered the aquahunters into the water, she and Dr Naunton began heated squabbles over every rock and pebble the machines filmed underwater. I didn't see loads of that, though; I was down the slope, fifty metres along the shore from Jessica, as we used the tablets to guide our submarines over the lakebed.

The rain was a constant smear, never hard but never-ending, and the shore soon became so boggy that I sank into it up to my shins. I didn't mind – the combat suit I'd been given was warm and waterproof – but the work was slow and tedious, and too much like archaeology for my liking.

After about an hour of searching, Pan rushed from the tent to check up on me. She didn't need to, but she was so excited she could barely stand still.

"Isn't this cool?" she asked breathlessly.

"I guess so," I replied, unconvinced.

"The Ninth Legion, Jake. This is proper archaeology, like Mum and Dad used to do."

"Mum and Dad were treasure hunters, Pan. And we're searching for the *key*, remember, not the legion. Saving the world, and everything?"

"Yeah, of course. But this is the right way to do it. After we find the key we can actually excavate the site, using coffer dams and underwater archaeology. Usually we just blow things up and rush off. Now we're doing it properly."

"Slowly, you mean?"

I'm not sure she heard my reply as she rushed back up the slope to the operations tent, and I was even less sure how Jessica heard from fifty metres away along the shore.

"Everything OK?" she yelled, squinting through the drizzle.

I shouted that it was, but suddenly she couldn't hear. She tapped her smart-goggles, signalling for me to put mine on too. When I did, Jessica's voice came through so clearly she could have been standing right next to me. We spoke as we continued controlling our submarines.

"Pan's a natural at this," she said. "Without her we'd never have got this far."

She was right. There wasn't a single day that I didn't feel lucky to have my sister on my side. But we needed to work faster.

"I know you're frustrated," she added. "But there's no faster way to locate the key. Except, of course... Actually, no, nothing."

I looked up from my control screen and wiped rain from my eyes. "Except what?"

"No, it was a stupid idea."

Now she *really* had my attention. Stupid ideas were my speciality. If there was even a chance it might speed up finding the key, surely it was worth considering.

"Let's say that we're talking hypothetically," I suggested.

She laughed, carried on operating her submarine. "OK, but *only* hypothetically, because it's far too reckless. It's just that the other times you needed to find a key, or escape something, you've been helped by the black smoke. Lord Osthwait thinks it's chosen you to help it become fully free of its prison. That's why it led you to the keys, and why it gives you visions of where you need to go with them all – the emerald door."

"But there's no way I'm helping it," I said. "And anyway, those times were because I turned the cogs on one of the keys. It caused all sorts of trouble."

"Exactly," she replied. "Totally stupid idea. I just remembered that was how you found the other keys. But this is a much better plan. Come on, let's keep at it before the weather gets even worse."

Looking back, I know that from that moment there was only one plan for me. I stayed on the lake shore for another hour or so, operating my submarine and trying to convince myself that Jessica was right, that Pan had this under control. But I knew what I was going to do – what I felt we had to do. It would take almost three weeks to search this lake using archaeology, and we weren't certain if this was even the right place to search. It was just a best guess.

We'd needed a proper plan, and now we had one.

## 29

I can't remember the excuse I gave Jessica to take a break, but she just smiled and said, "No problem". I was pretty sure that the People of the Snake wouldn't try to steal the keys back off me, but, just in case, I'd hidden my backpack in the boot of her Jeep under a bundle of duffel bags full of spare kit. I climbed the slope from the shore and trudged past the operations tent to the Jeeps parked off the track. So far the mercenaries had kept a keen eye on me, but now it was almost as if they'd been ordered *not* to look at me. I opened the boot of Jessica's Jeep and slid my backpack out.

I darted to the other side of the vehicle, so I was hidden from view, and leaned against the door, clutching the bag like a lifebelt as I considered what I was about to do. Pan had insisted that her plan would work. Maybe she was right. My grip loosened on the backpack. Maybe I should trust her...

"Hurry up, Jake!"

I flinched as Jessica's voice came through my goggles.

"This archaeology is going to take long enough even without you slacking off," she added. "If it even works..."

*Archaeology.*

My grip tightened again around the bag. I remembered my parents being swallowed by the black smoke, and my visions of the destruction of the lost civilization. I imagined the same happening today...

A knot tightened in my stomach, a sharp pain like a stitch. I unzipped the backpack, pulled out one of the keys and turned one of its crystal cogs.

"Jake?"

I flinched so suddenly that I dropped the key.

"Jake, what are you doing?" Pan asked.

I snatched the key up from the wet grass as my sister trudged closer. Had she seen what I'd done? Acting as cool as I could, I brought the key closer to my face, as if I had been inspecting its markings.

"Nothing much," I muttered. "Hoped to spot something on this that might speed things up."

"Oh," she replied, coming closer. "You didn't touch the cogs, though?"

I looked at her as if I wouldn't even dignify the question with an answer and shoved the key back into my bag. "Did anyone find anything yet?" I asked.

Pan hesitated, still suspicious about what I'd been doing, but then shook her head. "Not yet, but I reckon we'll have covered the area we expected to by the end of the day."

"Great," I said. "Only seventeen days left to go, then."

"Jake, if there's something here, we'll find it. This is the best way."

I nodded and smiled, even as the twist in my gut grew tighter. Right then I felt like I was on a different side to Pan, maybe even her enemy. But I shook the thought away. We were on the same side, even if we differed on how we should do things.

I was surprised to see Pan still hovering close by rather than rushing off to check up on the work. She only ever hovered when something was on her mind.

"What's up?" I asked.

"Nothing," she said. "I was just thinking."

"OK. About what?"

"Well, what next?"

"Oh. OK, if we find the key we'll then need to locate whatever door Marcus Turbo took them from, and–"

"No, I mean after that. After all of that. What next?"

Oh, *that* what next. I'd been so obsessed with finding the keys that I'd not really thought about what would happen if – *when* – we did. Or maybe I'd not *wanted* to think about it. Mum and Dad had come out of retirement for this mission. If we managed to save them, would they want to go back to our old home and boring old lives?

But maybe we wouldn't have to...

"Jessica says there are other missions," I said, "and that defeating the smoke thing isn't really the end of this for the People of the Snake."

"Yeah, but that's for them, Jake. Those are *their* missions. Anyway, I'm not sure I really want to be a treasure hunter. Charging around, blowing things up..."

"But that's what we do, right?"

"Not Dr Naunton, or Mum and Dad before all this. They were actual archaeologists and historians."

"You mean *books* and *libraries* and stuff?" I spat the words out as if they were poison. "That's not me, Pan."

She gave me that look again, chewing her lip, lost in faraway thoughts. "No," she agreed, finally. "But I think it's me."

She trudged back up the slope to the tent. I should have gone after her – I knew that brief exchange was the start of something heavier, but there was no time to worry about the future; I had to focus on what was happening right then.

I clutched the backpack even tighter to my chest, feeling my heart thump hard against it, and scanned the scraps of sky I could see between the swaying treetops. I had turned one of the key's cogs but... Nothing had happened. No black smoke, no new key. Nothing at all.

"Jake? Everything OK?"

Jessica's voice came through my smart-goggles again, snapping me from my skyward gaze. I turned, checked again around me, and then laughed. She was right – this had been a stupid idea. I shoved the bag back in the Jeep, and turned towards the lake.

And I stopped.

The lake... It was gone.

Where it had been now stretched an open heath dotted with granite boulders that jutted from the heather like ships sinking in a purple and pink sea. I turned and looked in the other direction. The operations tent had vanished, as well as the Jeeps and all the trees. The rain had stopped too. A few cotton wool clouds drifted lazily through an otherwise bright blue sky.

The key, the dials... The forest and lake had only existed in the last hundred years. Before that the area had looked like this. Was I back in Roman times again? If so, where were the Ninth Legion, the Praetorians and Marcus Turbo? And where would I find the key?

*"Thermal,"* I breathed.

The view in my goggles changed to a thermal image of the heath, fuzzy grey speckled with glowing orange blobs – the heat signatures of living things. These goggles were much better than my old ones, not only picking out heat signatures, but identifying them, too: *98% certainty rabbit, 96% certainty vole, 73% certainty fox...*

There was plenty of life out there, but none of it was human.

A trapdoor opened in my stomach, plunging panic. Had we got it wrong? I turned, scanning the hill that rose behind me, beyond where the operations tent had been. Weirdly, there were few orange blobs there, even though the slope was also covered in heather.

My pulse quickened. Why would there be so much wildlife on the heath but so little on that hill? Maybe those animals didn't like hills...

Or maybe something had scared them away.

The pulse reading on my lenses climbed even higher.

I set off up the hill, sinking knee-deep into heather that was soft on the top but thick and tangled beneath, and kept snagging on my boots. It felt as if I was picking my way through tangled nets. The slope grew steeper until I was almost scrambling, gripping handfuls of the heather to pull myself higher. A clump tore away in my hand and I tumbled several metres back down the slope, rolling over their springy tops.

I scrambled up and was about to laugh, when I heard a shout.

Actually, it was more like a roar, although I felt certain that it was human. The sound had come from the top of the hill, and it carried enough threat to make me want to continue my tumble down the slope. Instead, I sank even lower, trying to hide the heather. I heard it again, then again. It sounded like someone yelling a command, but not in English. Was it Latin? I wished Pan was with me; she'd understand it. But she wasn't – I'd betrayed her trust, and I didn't yet know what that would cost.

Jessica was right. So far the black smoke had helped me find the keys. Whatever was happening here, whatever I was being led towards, was for a reason.

I had to go on.

# 30

It took me another minute to gather enough courage to continue the slow climb up the hill. I stopped again near the crest, my blood refreezing with each wild cry that rang from the summit. There was no way I was going on until I knew what was up there. Luckily, my goggles had a useful new feature...

*"Periscope,"* I whispered.

The scene in my lenses changed to a view of the hilltop, and I lay on the heather staring at a scene that I could barely believe.

I had found the Ninth Legion.

Around five thousand Roman soldiers, spread as far as I could see across a wide hilltop plateau, were arranged into a V-shaped battle formation, a tight wedge protected on all sides by a wall of curved shields. Behind the shield bearers, legionaries gripped swords and daggers, shuffling with small steps across the heather as the whole formation advanced into battle.

Iron armour and bronze helmets gleamed in the sun.

Further back, Marcus Turbo watched from a horse. I recognized him from Morocco, although he now wore ceremonial armour, a red cape and a helmet topped with a curved red crest. He raised a staff that was mounted with a carved golden eagle, and roared an order, to which the legionaries responded with a deep, rhythmic war chant – *"Huh, huh, huh"* – urging one another on towards their enemy.

One enemy.

A wall of black smoke.

It rose fifty metres high, swirling and rolling like a storm cloud, moving slowly – almost teasingly – over the heather and towards the Roman army.

I wish I could tell you that I made a plan and acted fast and somehow saved all those soldiers. But I didn't. It was as if that instinct had been switched off. Instead I froze, staring, all of a sudden a coward.

"Run," I gasped. "Why don't you all run?"

But the soldiers were too brave, and too well trained, to flee.

How could something so silent and so weightless carry so much threat and cause such fear? I saw it in the legionaries' faces. Tough soldiers used to fighting savage tribes now looked utterly terrified – veins bulged in their necks and foreheads, teeth gritted, jaws clenched and eyes wild with fear as they continued their advance towards this faceless enemy.

Ahead of them, scattered across the heather

between the smoke and the soldiers, lay hundreds of Roman shields, sword, spears and helmets. I realized that the smoke had already taken the rest of the legion, leaving behind their weapons, like a monster spitting out its victims' bones.

The soldiers knew what awaited them, but still they advanced. They were only ten metres from the smoke now. I tried to cry out, but my mouth was too dry.

The general bellowed another order.

*"Huh, huh, huh,"* the soldiers chanted in reply.

I yanked off my smart-goggles. I couldn't watch any more. I covered my ears too, unable to bear the chanting. But another sound forced its way into them, so loud and so high that I heard it no matter how hard I clamped them shut.

The screams of five thousand soldiers.

And then, silence.

For a long moment I lay still, listening to my own frantic breathing and hammering heart. When I finally peeled my arms from my head and looked up, thin wisps of smoke fluttered over me, almost like dragonflies. They faded into grey and then vanished into the sunlight.

There were no cries, no screams. Was anyone even left?

Slowly, fearfully, I began to crawl over the heather and higher up the slope. This time I didn't use my goggles. Reaching the top of the hill, I rose on numb, shaky legs and looked around.

Only one figure remained on the battlefield, alone in the centre of the plateau. Marcus Turbo. He leaned against his staff; the imperial eagle at its top gleamed in the brilliant sunlight. He seemed injured, although he had no obvious wounds. Sweat gushed down his face, muscles strained in his arms and his legs trembled as if he was struggling to hold up some great weight.

Slowly, he raised his head and looked at me.

I almost turned and ran, but forced myself to scramble higher and move towards him. I might not have done had I not seen the leather satchel slung over his shoulder.

In it was the key.

As I approached, Turbo's mouth twisted into something like a smile, the scar creasing his cheek. I can't tell you how we spoke, whether I was speaking in Latin or he was in English, neither of which should have been possible. I only know that somehow we understood each other.

"I know you," he rasped.

It was all I could do to shake my head.

"Yes, I have seen you once, but I cannot think... Are you Roman?"

Another feeble head shake. I think I mumbled an apology too, although I'm not sure what for. "No, I'm just a boy," I stammered.

With a quivering arm, Turbo wiped sweat from his face so he could see me better.

"No," he grunted. "Not just a boy. You are here when everyone else is gone."

I stared around the hilltop. Where a whole legion had been only moments ago, now all I saw was the smoke fading to a thin, grey veil over the heather. Turbo thought I had survived this battle? That might have been funny if I wasn't so terrified.

His legs buckled and he sank to his knees. I reached to help him but held back, scared that he might suddenly lash out.

"Are you injured?" I asked.

"In a way," he groaned. "I do not have much time left."

"But ... why?"

"Tell me why you are here."

Warm wind swept across the hilltop, and a crow settled in the tree above, cawing with what sounded like disappointment. Perhaps it had seen the battle and expected bodies to peck at.

"I was sent here," I replied.

"By whom?"

If I told him the black smoke had sent me, I was sure he'd have found the strength to do something nasty to me with that sword around his waist. But I needed his satchel, so I needed his trust.

I cleared my throat and lowered my voice, hoping I'd sound brave.

"I have the other keys," I said. "The one you hid in the volcano in Morocco and the one from the ship you sent north. I also have one you don't even know about. Now I need the final key – the one you brought here."

His eyes stayed on me and widened with surprise. "How is this possible?" he croaked.

"Because I'm stronger than you and smarter than you."

It was a cocky reply, and a dangerous one.

"I do not understand," he said.

"You don't have to," I shot back. "All you need to know is that you should never have taken the keys. The black smoke, the force that just destroyed your army, is just a small part of something much more powerful, which is trying to escape its prison. If it does, it will destroy the whole world."

I considered trying to grab the satchel, but I'd have to wrestle it free and I *really* didn't fancy my chances in a fight with this guy.

He nodded slowly, gazing across the battlefield.

"Five thousand of the Empire's finest soldiers saw the smoke and now they are dead. You have seen it and you are alive. That is enough for me. So, boy, it falls to you to save the Empire."

It also didn't seem like a good idea to let him know about the collapse of the Roman Empire. "Yes," I agreed. "I need the key."

"There is one thing I ask," Turbo added. "Before your mission, take word of the fall of the Ninth Legion to Rome. It is vital that the Senate is informed."

He stood a fraction taller, still leaning on the eagle

staff for strength, and his eyes fixed on me with a laser-beam stare. It would have been easy to assure him that I would do what he asked, but it would be a lie. I sensed he was testing me.

"No," I replied. "I can't. My mission is my priority. Nothing else matters."

His eyes softened a little, and a slight smile cracked across his scarred face. Or perhaps it was a grimace. "Good," he rasped. "Good boy."

With what seemed to have been the last scraps of strength, he pulled his satchel over his shoulder. "The key is here. But first, tell me your name."

"Jake. My name is Jake Atlas."

"Well, Jake, I swore to protect these keys. Now that duty passes to you. Promise me you will never give up."

He coughed and slumped to his back on the heather. His eyes rolled, and the scar on his face darkened. And then I saw it.

The smoke again.

It came from his eyes in thin wisps, just like it had with the soldier in the chamber under Rome. I staggered back, watching, terrified, as a small, black cloud gathered over Marcus Turbo's body. It had been inside him the whole time we were talking. It had let him talk to me, and now it was going to swallow him.

Only...

"Wait," I gasped. "Where is the door? Mr Turbo? Wake up, I need to know where to find the door you took the keys from."

"It's... It's..."

Before he could finish, the black smoke dropped like a sheet, covering him completely.

"Jake? Jake, where are you?"

I whirled around in fright, but the voice had come through my smart-goggles. Pan sounded scared and desperate. Something was wrong, but I tried to ignore it, to focus on Turbo. Finding the keys was pointless unless we knew where to take them.

I ran at the small cloud of smoke and tried to clear it with my arms, swatting and kicking. "Get off him!" I cried. "Get off!"

But he was gone. It didn't make sense. The smoke wanted me to find the key; it needed me to. Why had it taken him before I had it?

"Jake? Jake!"

My sister needed me too. I turned to look back the way I had come. Rain lashed against my face, and then a gust of wind hit me so hard it sent me tumbling back. I hit a tree trunk, and then another as the wind slapped me to the side. I was back in the forest, fir trees swaying all around me. Above their tops, the clouds were so black it seemed like night. The visions were gone, and a storm had come.

I heard Pan scream again, and then Jessica yelling for me – both voices urgent in my smart-goggles – but I couldn't go back until I found the key. I'd never be able to tell where it was buried. I staggered to the spot where I thought Turbo had fallen, dropped to my knees and tore at the dirt with my fingers. If the smoke needed me to find that key, maybe it was just guiding me to it...

"Come on!" I cried. "It has to be here!"

The earth was too hard. I needed a digger or...

Or something even more powerful.

I picked myself up, sliding my goggles on as I staggered back.

*"Fire forward stun charge,"* I gasped.

A fizzing bolt of electricity fired from my goggles and struck the ground with an explosion of earth, stones and shattered tree roots. I wiped dirt from my eyes, hoping to see a huge crater, but the shot had only blasted a small hole in the forest floor. Desperate, I tore off my goggles, remembering another trick Jessica had taught me.

"Detonate, five seconds."

I tossed the goggles into the hole and staggered back, immediately wishing I'd given myself more time... I turned and leaped to the ground, covered my head with my arms, as the goggles detonated.

Considering the size of the goggles, the explosion they generated was incredible. It swept me up and flipped me into a cartwheel. I crashed against a tree and was showered with mud and stones from the blast. Something whacked against my head – something metal. I looked around, hardly able to see, and was just able to make out the bulbous shape of a bronze helmet lying a few feet away.

Marcus Turbo's helmet.

My ribs throbbed from the impact and my ears rang from the donation, but it had been worth the pain: the explosion had blasted a pond-sized crater between the trees. Wheezing, I scrambled closer on my hands and knees and shovelled mud from the pit. My hand hit another metal object. I pulled it from the ground, vaguely recognizing the shape of a sword, though two thousand years underground had left it looking more like a giant rusty nail. I kept digging, frantically scooping mud. I knew Turbo's satchel would have rotted away, so the key must be loose somewhere under all this dirt. I yanked up something made of bronze, vaguely aware that it was Turbo's imperial eagle, and then the skull of the Praetorian leader himself. I pushed both things away and dug harder until...

"Yes!" I screamed.

My hand struck on something that wasn't bone or armour, or any weapon. It felt like glass, or crystal. I lifted it from the pit, and held it up, letting the rain wash mud from the artefact. The key was undamaged. It seemed impossible in the dim light of the forest, but somehow the thing gleamed.

The skull in the pit appeared to grimace, as if suddenly regretting giving me the key. I wanted to say something to reassure him that I was the right person for this mission, but the fact was, I didn't know if that was true.

# 31

Clutching the key, I scrambled up and ran through the forest. Another rush of wind swept through the trees and sent me stumbling one way, then another. The storm was so fierce that it tore branches from the trees and sent them spinning overhead.

I reached the top of the slope and staggered back as if I'd been punched in the chest.

The storm had toppled trees on the slope, so I could see right down to the operations tent – or what was left of it. Wind had ripped it to shreds, smashed the holosphere tables and flipped several Jeeps over onto their sides. Fierce gusts lashed across the lake surface, sweeping up waves that crashed over the shore. But that wasn't what I stared at. In the middle of the lake, the wind had sucked the water into a dark, spinning funnel that rose as high as I could see into the sky. A twister – and it was moving towards the shore.

I spotted mercenaries on the banks, battered from all sides by wind and flying branches as they fled to the forest.

"Pan!" I screamed.

I could just see her, crouching with Jessica behind one of two Jeeps that the storm hadn't overturned. But my cry was lost in the wind, and without my goggles I had no other way of calling to her.

I shoved the key in my pocket and charged down the hill. The rain hit my face so hard that it became impossible to see. A clash of thunder boomed above the trees, as if someone had fired a cannon over my head. I fell to the ground, covering my ears, as it boomed again. I'd never heard a noise like it.

I rose and ran as wind and rain slapped and shoved me from tree to tree like a pinball. I tumbled over, staggered up, and kept moving until I reached Pan and Jessica.

I slid up beside Pan and we grabbed each other in a quick hug, each relieved to see the other safe. The wind off the lake was so fierce that the Jeep kept jolting, like it was being battered by the Hulk.

Pan drew her knees to her chest, shivering and gasping. "When will this stop?" she demanded.

"We don't know," Jessica replied.

"You have all this super high-tech kit," Pan yelled, "but you can't get a weather report to find out when a storm will pass?"

"No, you don't understand. There is no storm."

"What?"

"According to every report the skies should be clear. There is no natural explanation for all this."

Pan looked as confused as she was scared, but the information didn't surprise me. I knew what had happened. It was the god. I knew because I had caused this. Guilt stabbed at my chest, but I tried to ignore it, reminding myself again that my plan had worked. We had the key. Now we needed a new plan.

"This Jeep's flooded, but I can get it started," Jessica hollered. "Maybe we can escape."

No!" I yelled back, "we need to reach *that* Jeep over there. The other keys are in the back."

I pointed across the shore to the vehicle in which I'd stashed my bag. The shore there was totally flooded, and lake water had risen halfway up the Jeep.

"What are you all talking about?" Pan shouted. "We still have a mission. We still have to find the final key. It's still out there somewhere, in the lake."

"The key's not in the lake, Pan."

"Jake, I know you don't like—"

"No, I mean I have it." I yanked Turbo's key from my pocket, and showed it to her.

Pan stared at the artefact as if it was a more astonishing sight than the huge twister.

"I... Where was it?" she asked.

"It was just lying on the ground. I got lucky."

Even among all the chaos of the storm, I felt another stab of guilt. At any other time she would have given me one of her probing looks, searching my face for evidence of the lie she knew I'd just told. But there was no time. We had the key, so now we had to survive.

The whirlwind was now as high and wide as a skyscraper, a spinning monster that had turned the whole lake into a vortex, like the most enormous amount of water swirling down a plughole. It was moving towards the shore.

Mercenaries staggered past, fleeing from the twister. The wind was so fierce it swept one of them up and tossed him twenty metres through the rain. Even so, they had the right idea. We had to get away, too – but not without the keys.

"Stay here," I cried. "I'll get the keys."

"No!" Jessica yelled. "We all go. I can get that Jeep moving."

"It's half sunk in water," Pan shouted.

"It's amphibious," Jessica said. "Let's go!"

She led the way, crouched against the driving rain. Pan and I followed, huddled together as the wind tried to batter us back. Soon the floodwater was too deep to wade through, so we swam for the Jeep. The twister was a hundred metres away, but I could feel its force, a tugging current I had to fight against.

Pan shouted, "Jake, where did you find that key?"

"Keep moving!" I yelled, pretending not to hear.

The Jeep was now submerged up to its windows. Jessica tried to open the driver's door, but the water pressure was too strong. Pan and I swam alongside her, grabbed the handle and together we forced the door open.

"Get in!" Jessica shouted.

We bundled into the back seats. So much water flooded in that we were floating more than sitting. In the front, Jessica fumbled with the control panel until – miraculously – the engine spluttered to life. Despite being almost totally submerged, the Jeep actually began to drive. It wasn't fast, but we were moving.

"Yes!" I yelled.

I looked to Pan, expecting her to share my delight that maybe we could actually get out of this. But she just stared at me with narrow, suspicious eyes.

"How did you find the key, Jake?"

"What?"

"You heard me!"

"I told you, it was lying on the ground. The tornado must have pulled it up. Who cares, anyway? We have it. We have them all, Pan."

I leaned over the back seats, found my backpack floating among the sodden kitbags and pulled it free. I grinned, showing it to Pan, and shoved Turbo's key in with the others. Though we had all four keys, Pan didn't look happy. She was about to say something else, but Jessica yelled from the driver's seat.

"Get your seatbelts on! It's coming!"

The great funnel of wind and water, now as black as the storm clouds overhead, had reached the shore. It was close enough to glimpse tree trunks, and even large fish, spinning in its vast bulk. The lake water began to suck back, pulling our Jeep towards the twister. The vehicle creaked and shunted, fighting against the drag.

"You call this high-tech?" Pan screamed at Jessica. "I could swim faster!"

We'd reached the slope to the forest road, but the Jeep struggled to climb it, tugged in the other direction by the force of the whirlwind and the current. The whole vehicle shuddered as we rose, slowly, up the short, steep hill.

"Pan, hold your breath!" I hollered.

Water rushed from the front of the Jeep to the back, submerging me and my sister. We held our breath, praying we'd reach the top of the bank before our lungs ran out of air. The engine revved and roared as Jessica shifted gears and stamped on the accelerator. Finally the Jeep drove onto the bank and lake water gushed out the windows.

We skidded along the track between the trees as Jessica struggled to control the Jeep. Behind, the twister loomed larger, closer. A warning flashed on the Jeep's windscreen. DANGER – IMMINENT THREAT FROM REAR.

"We know that!" Jessica yelled.

"Can't you stop it?" Pan called.

It took me a moment to realize she was talking to me. "What?"

"It likes you, doesn't it?" she replied. "It's using

you to get fully free. So why is it trying to kill you?"

"Maybe it's not!" Jessica shouted. "Maybe it's just trying to get rid of the rest of us, so we can't stop Jake from freeing it."

"Is that true?" Pan demanded, glaring at me.

"How do I know?" I yelled, angry at the accusation in her eyes. "It's not my friend! Watch out!"

Jessica yanked the steering wheel as a sapling ripped from the forest floor and flew over the Jeep, its roots slapping the windscreen. The spinning monster was one hundred metres back, tearing up trees on either side of the forest track and tossing them into the air as if they were blades of grass.

"Drive faster!" Pan demanded.

"We can't," Jessica grunted. "The tyres can't get a grip in this mud. We've miles before we hit the road."

"Does this Jeep have laser blasters?" I asked.

"Yes."

"Then use them! Cut through the forest, blast the trees!"

Pan yelled something in protest, but Jessica was already on it. As we turned from the path and into the forest, electrolaser blasts fired from the front of the Jeep. The shots hit a tree in our path with an explosion of sparks that strobe-lit the dark woodland. The tree toppled forward and the Jeep jolted as we drove over the fallen trunk. Jessica fired again and again, toppling more trees to clear a path. One of the shots missed its target, but she reacted fast, turning the Jeep so we slammed into the trunk from the side. The impact thrust us across the seats, causing my head to clash against Pan's.

We hit another trunk, skidded and crashed into a third. Each impact sent us tumbling across the seats. It felt like someone was using my skull as a football, but we were getting closer to the road. The sky was so dark from the storm that the street lights had come on, and they weren't far away.

Jessica yanked the gear stick and accelerated, firing laser bolts at more trees in our way. We burst onto the road among a storm of sparks, shattered wood and driving rain.

"Jake, what now?" she hollered.

The twister was still coming. It was spinning as high as I could see into the sky, tearing up trees in its path. As I stared, I suddenly felt deflated. How did we stand a chance – three of us in a smashed-up Jeep against a *god*?

I sank in the seat, clutched my backpack and groaned. Pan grabbed one of my arms and dug her nails into my skin.

"Hey!" she insisted. "We need a plan!"

"I don't have one!" I snapped.

"That's not good enough! You brought this thing here, so get rid of it."

I glared at her. "What does *that* mean?"

Jessica turned the Jeep along another country road and I slid across the seat into Pan. My sister shoved me away.

"Don't think I don't know," Pan said. "I saw you. You moved the cogs so the god would lead you to the final key. You had to do it *your* way."

I knew she knew, but it was still a shock to hear her accuse me of betraying her trust. She was right, but that didn't mean I was wrong.

"Your plan was too slow, Pan."

"We would have found the key eventually," she insisted.

"How long is that? Weeks? Months? How long do you want to wait to save Mum and Dad?"

"But we'd have done it *our* way, without *that*."

She pointed to the tornado. It had reached the road, where it ripped asphalt from the surface like it was tearing off a scab. It was still coming after us, growing larger with every mile. An electricity pylon leaned towards the spinning tower, struggling to cling to the ground. In an explosion of sparks it tore from its foundations and spun into the sky, yanking power cables with it into the whirlwind.

"*Look* at it, Jake," Pan said. "You have no idea the cost of letting it out. We'd have found the key, and the door too, Jake. We could have done it without all this destruction, like Mum and Dad would have wanted. Instead you've done it *their* way."

Now she was pointing at Jessica.

"What?" I asked.

"Come on, Jake," she said, "they've been using you."

"We're working with them..."

"You know why Mum and Dad came out of retirement? Because they wanted to stop the People of the Snake from destroying the things they found. They would never have wanted us to team up with them."

"We needed to, Pan..."

"No, we didn't! They used us. Why do you think they had suits ready for us, exactly our size, and smart-goggles too? And I bet your idea to find the final key didn't come from nowhere. *She* put it in your head, didn't she?"

Another finger jab towards Jessica.

"Sorry, Jake," Jessica said. "We needed to speed things up."

"You used me?" I asked.

"We needed your help and we knew how to get it. You should be flattered. We've never put so much effort into recruiting anyone. Look, you two can squabble all you want when this is over, but right now we have a tornado chasing us. We're almost back at Vindolanda. If Osthwait made it too, there will be helicopters coming. We might still get out of this alive, and with all the keys."

It was our best shot, but I swore at her anyway. The Pan and I sat in silent sulks, both staring out of the window as the beginning of the end of the world raged outside.

# 32

None of us said another word as we raced the final few miles back to Hadrian's Wall. Jessica took the most direct route, smashing through hedgerow and speeding across a field. The tornado tore after us, ripping up a farm shed and then reducing a country pub to rubble, as it continued its relentless chase. I strapped my backpack on as we turned down the driveway to Vindolanda Fort.

"End of the line," Jessica called. "Let's go!"

We skidded to a stop, leaped from the Jeep and sprinted to the visitor centre. The whole building was shaking as if it had a fever. Tiles flew from the roof and were sucked up by the approaching whirlwind. It took all my strength to hold the door open as Pan and Jessica charged in. I should have followed, but for a moment I stood, staring up at the tornado through the rain, as fascinated by the sight as I was terrified. It had turned jet black, a spinning funnel so wide that it was impossible to see anything other than its vast swirling bulk. It was a few hundred metres away, tearing up trees and rocks from the countryside, but it wasn't moving any closer. It seemed to have paused, like it was waiting for something.

Was it, somehow, watching me?

I let go of the door and stepped towards the spinning tower, staring up at it through the rain. I was ready to grab a drainpipe to stop the whirlwind pulling me closer, but I didn't need to. Now that I was alone with it, I no longer felt any of its force. The twister still raged, sucking up Jeeps and electricity pylons further away, but I felt nothing.

It was sparing me.

Suddenly it was as if the storm had swept inside me, a raging fury...

"What do you want?" I screamed. "I'm not going to help you. I won't!"

My cry was lost to the roar of the twister and the shatter of tiles flying from the roof. The tornado began to move again, spinning even closer to the visitor centre, closer to me. It was no longer made up of wind or rain or lake water. It was smoke, a vast tower of black smoke, in which a shape was beginning to form. Glaring eyes. A cruel, grinning mouth. It was watching me. And laughing.

"Jake! Get in!"

Pan and Jessica rushed from the centre. Pan

grabbed my arm, and together they dragged me back through the entrance. A few mercenaries pulled the door shut and jammed a broomstick through the handle to stop the wind from tearing it open.

I turned, breathing hard and wiping wet hair from my face. About a dozen mercenaries had made it back here, soaked and shattered from the effort. I was relieved to see that Dr Naunton had made it too. He sat wrapped in a blanket, staring out a window with a sad, lost gaze. His site – his life – was being torn to shreds.

Lord Osthwait stood in the centre of the room looking totally unruffled. His hair was still perfectly slicked back, his suit uncreased. Even his moustache had kept its perfectly positioned twirls.

He accepted a mug of tea from Betty, sipped it as calmly as if he were at a village fete and gave her an appreciative nod.

"Perfect," he said.

Betty smiled – despite everything, she seemed genuinely happy with the compliment. One last cup of tea before the end of the world.

A window shattered. Wind howled through the room, toppling a cabinet and sending maps and papers flapping into the air like panicked birds. Betty rushed to gather them up, but no one else moved.

"So what now?" Pan asked.

"Well," Lord Osthwait said, setting his mug down, "I would like to say this is our last stand but, alas, there is no stand to make. We are simply waiting."

"Waiting for what?"

"For whatever that is outside to take us."

"But what about helicopters, a rescue team?" Pan demanded. "You have unlimited resources, remember?"

"We do, but that thing outside would destroy any attempt at a rescue. The helicopter pilots would almost certainly die."

"But you must have a plan?"

"We have hundreds of plans, Miss Atlas. However, none are for stopping a god."

"So... We're just going to wait for that thing to take us all?"

"Not all," Jessica replied. "It will leave one of us behind."

"Ah, yes," Osthwait agreed. He picked up his tea, sipped it again, and then looked at me and smiled. "I trust you will not be too lonely, Master Atlas."

I knew what he meant, but I refused to believe it. Just because that thing outside wanted me to help set it free, didn't mean I had to, or would.

"No," I insisted. "It's got nothing to do with me."

"That's not true, Jake," Jessica said. "Think about everything you've done in the past year. You found the emerald tablets. You found all four keys. Maybe the god has been using you the whole time."

"Shut up!" I snapped. "That's not true. You were after those tablets and the keys too. We just beat you to them."

"Indeed," Osthwait agreed, "but think about all of the destruction that caused. You caused. That thing out there lives for such chaos. It sees in you its perfect partner. It is using your considerable talents to its advantage. You found the keys, and now it plans to use you to help it become fully free. It has shown you how, and you have followed its instructions, albeit unknowingly. I suspect now it will lead you to the door to use the keys to release it from its prison. And then all of the chaos it has caused so far will seem a mere warm-up for the revenge it will take upon humanity."

I didn't want to accept it, but I knew it was true, at least partly. The god had put ideas in my head, and I had acted them out. I had always thought I had a skill at making plans, finding lost artefacts, but was it ever really me? It hadn't even pushed me; all I'd needed was a nudge. It had used my nature – impulsive, rash, destructive – to its advantage. I was on its side, even though I'd never known it, or wanted to be. That had led to my parents being taken, and caused me to break my promise to them. It had led us here, to this shaking visitor centre, where the only thing left that I loved – my sister – was about to be taken too.

I didn't know how to stop it.

I was out of plans.

"The only hope I can offer now is a telephone number," Osthwait continued. "Call one-one-six-nine, then hang up. Wait exactly three minutes, then call two-two-seven-nine and give your name to whoever answers. That is a contact for our organization. They will know who you are and will come to collect you. Perhaps they will be able to work out the location of the door, where you need to go with those keys. If so, they will prepare a small army to accompany you on the mission."

The visitor centre roof shuddered and then part of it tore away and spun up into the sky. Rain and wind lashed into the room, sending more papers flying. I grabbed Pan, and we huddled beside Dr Naunton as the walls began to shake and another window shattered. Through the broken glass we saw the tornado tear up Hadrian's Wall – two thousand years of history simply peeled from the ground. I expected to see the ancient stones fly up into the swirling tower, but instead a long section of the Wall rose and curled up, and then lashed at the visitor centre like a whip. It crashed against the front doors, shattering them, and then shot back and struck the building again, causing bricks to crumble.

We staggered back, dragging Dr Naunton with us. He just stared silently at the destruction of the monument to which he'd dedicated his whole life.

Through the broken doors I saw the twister move even closer. It whipped Hadrian's Wall at us again, causing more of the centre's walls to crumble, as the last of the roof flew up into the storm. It was taking the place apart bit by bit.

Pan grabbed my arm. "Jake!" she yelled. "Whatever happens, don't do what it wants."

"I'm not going to, Pan. Nothing's going to happen! I can think of a plan..."

"Jake, listen to me! We should never have come here. We should never have broken our promise to Dad."

"That wouldn't have made a difference..."

"Yes, it would have! *You* wouldn't have been here, Jake. Osthwait's right, it was using you. It's going to take us, but not you."

"No, Pan, I won't let it. I can think of–"

"Just listen, will you! Promise me you won't come after me. Don't do what it wants. Promise me what you promised Dad, and this time keep your word."

No. She couldn't ask that. "Pan, I can't... I can save you, and Mum and Dad."

"Jake, that's what it wants. It *wants* you to take the keys to the door. Then it will *make* you set it free."

"I won't let it, Pan."

Behind us, another wall collapsed. I heard screams, and caught glimpses of mercenaries being sucked into the sky by the whirlwind. I saw Dr Naunton, still barely aware of what was going on, slide across the floor and then suddenly shoot up into the spinning darkness. I think Lord Osthwait and Jessica went then too, and even poor Betty, but I didn't see them go or hear their cries. My eyes were locked on Pan, and hers on me. She gripped my arm even harder as the whirlwind began to tug at her back.

Still the storm didn't seem to affect me at all. All this chaos was happening around me, and I could barely even feel it.

"Jake," she insisted, "promise me."

I grabbed her arms and clung on, struggling to keep hold. Her eyes were full of fear, but they were also fierce and determined, fixed on me.

*"Promise me!"*

I wanted to reply, but I didn't know what to say. How could I promise that? I pulled her closer and held onto her with all my strength, as the whirlwind smashed the last of the visitor centre walls to rubble and tried to tear my sister from my arms. I heard her demand again that I make the promise, but I turned my head, looking for something, anything, that might anchor us to the ground.

"Pan," I shouted, "that sink! If we can reach it–"

I didn't know how the sink would have helped us, and we never got to find out. At that moment, the tornado tore my sister from my grasp, ripping her away so violently that I didn't even see her go.

"Pan!" I cried.

I yelled her name again and again, then sat alone among the visitor centre ruins, gasping and crying as the tornado continued to swirl fifty metres away beyond the rubble. Lord Osthwait, Jessica, Mum, Dad and now Pan. I'd lost them all.

No... I could get her back. I *had* to.

I scrambled up and ran, leaping over piles of bricks

and through the shattered remains of the building's front doors. The tornado was now twenty metres away, whisking the rubble of the visitor centre into its spinning funnel. I should have been sucked in too – I was closer than any of the others had been – but still the storm spared me.

"Pan!" I screamed.

Was she still there, somewhere in the black smoke? The tornado wasn't going to pull me in, but it couldn't stop me from *going* in. Screaming, I charged for the spinning tower, ready to be swept up into the vortex. I'd need every scrap of skill and quick thinking to keep focused and look for my sister as the tornado spun me around...

I ran harder, but just as I was about to hit the tornado the smoke parted, forming an arched entrance that closed up the moment I stumbled through. I stood, chest heaving, right in the centre of the twister.

"No..." I rasped.

I ran again at the smoke, but again it parted, letting me out of the funnel.

"No!"

I turned and ran at it again, and again I staggered into the centre of the funnel. I stared up at the spinning tower of smoke that rose all around me and yelled my sister's name until my voice ran dry. Then I sank to my knees in the middle of the twister, breathless and defeated.

I slumped lower, put my head in my hands and

cried. Actually, I sobbed. I'd lost the most important thing in the world: my family.

It took me a few minutes to realize I was no longer in the centre of the tornado. When I looked again, through eyes blurry with tears, the twister had begun to vanish. Wisps of black smoke flapped around me, like hundreds of crows taking flight. They dissipated and disappeared into a sky so bright that it stung my eyes after the darkness of the storm.

Everything around me had been destroyed. Hadrian's Wall, the visitor centre – the entire countryside was ripped up and devastated. Every car was gone, every power line and tree. The storm had left me unhurt, but I felt as if it had swept right inside me and torn me to shreds.

It had beaten me, and taken everything – except for one thing.

I pulled my backpack off and dropped it to the sodden ground. It was soaked with rain and felt heavier than ever. I heard the four keys bash against one another inside. The fate of the entire world sat in that bag. But, right then, that meant nothing to me compared with the fate of my family.

The storm was gone, but inside me it raged fiercer than ever. I stared at the last wisps of smoke fading in the bright blue sky.

"You think I'm going to help you?" I gasped. "I'm going to *destroy* you."

# 33

It took me eight hours to reach home from the north of England. I had no money, but a year of learning the sneaky skills of treasure hunting turned out to be useful for fare dodging too. Actually, I can't remember much of the journey. My body went into autopilot, getting me to the only place I could think to go. I stared out of the train window, not thinking at all. I couldn't let myself think, scared that the reality of what happened might overwhelm me. I didn't say a word or look at anyone. I didn't notice the sun set or night fall, or even that my clothes were still damp from the storm.

I got out at the nearest station to my home and walked in a daze. I passed my old school and the one Pan had gone to for gifted students, the one she used to call the "freak-show school". She had hated the place. She was always so far ahead of even the most talented students that there was no challenge.

I remembered how excited she'd been before the storm, leading the archaeology hunt, squabbling with Dr Naunton. The sparkle in her eyes...

I walked faster, not looking back.

It was late afternoon by the time I reached home. My family's house sat at the end of a cul-de-sac of identical houses, with identical-looking estate cars parked in their identical driveways. I triggered the security light's sensor and it dazzled my aching eyes. A year ago, that light had seemed pretty high-tech. That was before I learned about holospheres and smart-goggles and stuff like that.

A police sign on our front door warned visitors that the building was a crime scene and shouldn't be entered. I tore it down and went inside.

Mum would totally have freaked out if she'd seen how badly the police – or maybe the People of the Snake's mercenaries, who were really in charge – had messed the place up. Books had been torn from shelves, clothes tipped from drawers and family photographs yanked from the walls. I guessed the organization had been looking for a secret treasure-hunting headquarters – some clues to help them catch us. But Mum and Dad had moved here to escape that old life. They'd not left any secrets to find.

Despite everything, I couldn't help smiling to think of the mercenaries having to report their failure back to Lord Osthwait, as well as the scandal the whole thing must have caused around the cul-de-sac. Years ago, one of the neighbours had borrowed another's wheelbarrow without asking. The incident became the talk of the neighbourhood, by far the most exciting thing that had ever happened here. Since then, the residents had had to deal with the fact that their neighbours – a whole family of us – were wanted international terrorists.

I went upstairs to my sister's room, where I stood and stared at the posters of heavy metal bands that covered every inch of the walls. Each had an over-the-top name – Death Kill, Sons of Satan, Hangman's Noose – scrawled in black gothic lettering and accompanied by pictures of skulls, pentagrams and red-faced demons bursting out of drums. They reminded me of the carvings in temples we'd discovered, crossed with a cheap Halloween show. I never understood the difference between one heavy metal band and another. It was all just mad guitars and screaming. I hated it, and suspected that sometimes Pan did too, and that she only played it so often, and so loud, to annoy me.

But right then I was desperate to hear it again.

Pan insisted the only way to listen was on vinyl, so Mum and Dad had given her a second-hand record player for her birthday. It took me a few minutes to work out how to use it, but eventually the thrash music was blaring so loudly it caused the speakers to vibrate.

"Heavy metal, thrash metal and death metal all mean different things, Jake," my sister had once yelled, before slamming her door and cranking the music to full volume.

To me they all meant the same thing.

Pan.

I sat on her bed, listening as long as my eardrums could handle it, then turned the volume down and left her room.

For several hours I sat in the kitchen, scoffing whatever food I found in the cupboards that could still be eaten: cold baked beans, tuna, tinned tomatoes, canned sweetcorn. None of it was nice, especially cold, but I just kept eating, not even thinking. A pack of stale Hobnobs, half a jar of peanut butter. Afterwards, I felt sick and realized that I'd not really wanted to eat anything at all. What I had felt, what I had been trying to fill, wasn't hunger. It was emptiness, and I felt it more acutely now than ever.

I stared out the window at our little back garden, at the bird table scattered with mouldy bread crumbs and the rickety shed at the back of the lawn, where Mum and Dad had spent hours potting plants. I think they went there to escape me and Pan squabbling, because they were pretty rubbish gardeners. You might think that the garden looked untended and overgrown because we'd been away for so long, but really it was always a mess.

But it was our mess. Our garden. Our family.

I kept staring out the window as dusk turned into night, the birds fell silent and the garden and the shed and the mess were swallowed by darkness.

Then I went to bed.

# 34

I saw it again that night in my dream.

The emerald door. The four keys glowing, pulsing, beckoning me closer.

The city being destroyed, and the fires and the rockslides and the end of a civilization.

The black smoke drifting even closer, and in its swirling vastness the grinning face and the glowing red eyes.

I heard her, too. My sister, screaming.

*"Save me. Please, Jake, save me from this!"*

I woke, staring up at the bedroom ceiling. My heart was beating so fast I felt like someone was in the room, sneaking up on me in the dark.

"Pan?" I gasped. "Mum? Dad?"

I scrambled to the bedside table and turned on a light.

There was no one there.

I was still alone. They were still gone.

I sat back on the bed, clutching my chest, trying to fight the panic that was sweeping over me like a tsunami.

They needed me.

I had to save them, had to try.

But... I had made a promise.

Beside the bed, my backpack sat on the ground.

# 35

I didn't sleep at all after the dream, although I stayed in bed, staring at the ceiling, until the first light crept around the curtains and I heard birds begin their morning chatter. I jumped out of bed, ran downstairs and stood by the telephone.

Only one thing was on my mind: Lord Osthwait's final words.

*"Call one-one-six-nine, then hang up. Wait exactly three minutes, then call two-two-seven-nine and give your name to whoever answers."*

I could call for help. I had once been inside the People of the Snake's headquarters, so I knew that Osthwait was just one of several council members who led the organization. There were other senior people, clever people in command of mercenaries and able to recruit top historians and archaeologists. Osthwait had promised that they would prepare a small army to join me on a mission to defeat the god and save my family.

I reached for the phone but my hand stopped half-way, trembling.

*I* had promised something too.

I felt so heavy, like a great weight was pressing on me from above, and I had to sit down.

I'd never felt so confused or lost. What should I do? I had no one to ask. For some reason I remembered the old wise man in Kathmandu, croaking meaningless gibberish. I wished he was with me then; I'd take any advice at all.

*Had* his words been so meaningless, though, when he warned me that a cycle of destruction had begun? I had thought he'd meant the destruction of the lost civilization and how it might happen again. But was he talking more directly to *me*? The destruction that I brought about every time I went on a mission? The destruction that the god had *wanted* me to cause, to help it become free?

*Promise me, Jake. Promise me!*

I groaned, stared out the window at the garden, trying to calm my swirling mind. Maybe some fresh air would help me decide what to do. A walk in our messy little garden might...

I sat up.

"Our messy little garden," I muttered.

Somewhere, deep in the back of my mind, a tiny alarm began to sound.

I rose and went out. The sun had barely risen, it was chilly and the overgrown grass was soaked with dew, but I didn't notice any of that. I turned, gazing around the flower borders, which were now home to hundreds of weeds, but where no flowers had ever been planted.

So what were my parents always doing in that shed?

I'd never even thought to wonder. They were usually either working in their stuffy upstairs study or tinkering in the potting shed, while I was watching TV or reading comics, not at all interested in what they were up to. But I knew them differently now. Now, I did wonder, and it didn't make any sense.

I trudged through the wet grass to the shed. Its only window was speckled with green algae and a strip of roofing felt hung down.

I opened the door and peered inside.

Darkness, spider webs. Against one of the walls stood Mum's and Dad's bikes, on which they'd cycled to the college most mornings. Against the other was a long workbench, scattered with clay pots and a few other gardening bits and bobs. Everything was musty and dusty and stank of damp.

"Mum, Dad," I whispered to myself, "what did you do in here?"

The door creaked behind me as I stepped inside, my senses growing sharper every second as my parents' training kicked in. They hadn't taught me and

Pan anything about garden sheds, but we'd had *many* lessons on how to think when entering lost tombs.

*Look for anything out of place, anything that doesn't seem quite right. Use all your senses.* Feel *the space.*

I breathed in, held the breath and let it go again, calming my mind. I stepped deeper among the clutter and stopped.

The door creaked again.

But the floorboards did not creak at all.

I crouched, startling a huge spider. As I watched it scuttle, first between the floorboards and then back up and away into the corner, the alarm grew louder in my head. The spider wasn't able to escape between the boards because there was something under there blocking its way. It was strange, too, that this area of the shed floor was so tidy when everything else in here was such a mess. I rose, gazing around the darkness.

*Look for anything out of place...*

There.

That plant pot on the workbench.

If my parents didn't do any gardening in here, why does that plant pot have a fern in it? And how was it still alive? I doubted any of the neighbours had been popping round to water it.

I edged closer. It *looked* real.

I touched it.

It was plastic.

I'll admit, after that I got lucky. I only meant to

pick the pot up to inspect it. I had no idea that it was a trigger for a secret door. As I lifted it from the workbench, something tugged at its base – a lever that ran through the surface, cranking a hidden mechanism under the bench. I staggered to the side as, behind me, a small door rose from the floor, inviting me down into the darkness beneath.

"Whoa," I gasped.

I'd seen quite a few secret doors over the past year, and this was both the least impressive and the most surprising. I mean, I'd come to expect secret doors in tombs and temples. But in my parents' potting shed? I'd lived in this house my whole life, and had had no idea. They'd kept it a total secret, which meant they didn't want me going down there.

So, of course I went down.

I must have triggered a sensor as I went down the steps, because a light came on, illuminating a small subterranean chamber. The chilly underground air reeked of mould. I edged further down, cautious in case my parents had rigged the chamber with traps. I began to wonder if my parents had actually retired from treasure hunting or if the whole time they had been college professors they'd still been charging off on missions to save artefacts for museums. I was expecting something high-tech, an operations base like those the People of the Snake set up everywhere, but it wasn't quite that. There was a large holosphere screen and a chair, but that was all, other than several bookshelves crammed with notebooks. There were no weapons, no combat suits, not a single bit of high-tech action kit. Just the screen and the notebooks.

As I gazed around the small space, I realized that this wasn't an operations base at all. Mum and Dad had come out of retirement last year because they'd discovered what the People of the Snake were up to and couldn't ignore that. This must have been where they'd found out, where they'd kept an eye on the world of their past lives. So what were all these notebooks?

I slid one of them from its place on a shelf and flicked through. It was a diary full of handwritten notes by Mum.

*19 May 1996*

*Tomorrow we set off to locate the tomb of Genghis Khan. We expect traps, rival hunters and temperatures well below freezing, but nothing that we have not encountered before, and we are prepared. We are on the verge of one of the greatest archeological finds in history, so why do I feel so apprehensive? Years ago, as a student, I dreamed of such a discovery. But not like this. Even if we beat our rivals to the tomb, John and I expect to have a matter of hours to remove whatever artefacts we can, so they can be preserved in a museum rather than sold on the black market. Hours! Such a find deserves years of study, by a dozen experts. Instead it must be another "smash and grab job", as John so eloquently puts it. We have no choice, of course, if we wish to preserve any of this history for study. But is this archaeology? If only there was more time!*

I flicked ahead several pages, scanning densely written accounts of an expedition to Mongolia. There were sketches of artefacts, measurements, detailed descriptions of architecture and photographs of geological features that my parents had encountered along the way. The notebook was a meticulous archaeological report.

I closed it, took another from a different shelf and read an entry at random.

*6 January 1998*

*The Spear of Destiny! I cannot believe I'm actually writing those words! The lance that pierced the side of Jesus Christ as he hung on the cross. A year ago I would have thought such a thing to be mere mumbo jumbo, much like the Holy Grail or the Ark of the Covenant, another wild goose chase for fantasists, not archaeologists. But there is real, compelling evidence to suggest this spear exists and can be found. And what a find it would be! What a piece of history! Every element of this search should be recorded, documented and made available for scrutiny by top experts in biblical history. But, once again, that is not possible. Again, we are in a race. Another smash and grab job.*

*Big scream.*

*What we do is important, but it feels so distant to what we* once *did. What I would give for the time to do this properly!*

The notebook was crammed with more photos, sketches and lengthy descriptions of every aspect of their mission. Mum's voice rang so clear in my head, as if she was standing beside me reading out loud. I remembered what Professor Elena had said at the museum, that she had never seen such passionate historians as my parents when they were younger. She had known Mum and Dad as academics, not treasure hunters.

Mum had kept these diaries as records. That at least had been something she could control, something she could do – as she put it – *properly*. It was the same word Pan had used at the lake. She had been so excited to have time to find the key on her terms. But I'd wrecked all that.

I'd smashed and grabbed.

I flicked through other notebooks, pulling out one after another, scanning dates, searching. Finally I found an entry from the date I was looking for: a year before Pan and me were born. That was around the time Mum and Dad had retired as treasure hunters and moved here. The pages crumpled a little under my fingers, and I realized how hard I was gripping the book. My heart was picking up speed too, as if someone was spying on me. But I needed to know what had been going on in my parents' heads.

I sat at the holosphere table, and read.

*And so it ends, our time as... Well, as whatever John and I have been for the past decade. I cannot say that we have been historians or archaeologists. That would be a discredit to those who do that magnificent work, those who toil in libraries rather than lost tombs. I will not lie, however, and claim that we have not enjoyed parts of the work. I will never forget the discoveries we have made and the thrill of those moments. I believe that, ultimately, we have been a force for good. I have to believe that! There are now important artefacts in museums, available for academic study, which would otherwise have been sold on the black market and never been seen again, although we have sworn to never divulge which artefacts in particular. So, there is that to cling onto. But, as much as we have saved we have ruined. Our rivals thought nothing of destroying anything in the way of their prize. Had we not been there to challenge them, would they have been so destructive? Would it have all been so smash and grab?*

*Huge, huge sigh.*

*I know only this much: we are tired. We will keep an eye on the black market in case there are any missions that simply cannot be ignored. But I struggle at this moment to think of anything that would bring us out of retirement.*

*There should not be a difference between treasure*

*hunting and archaeology. But, sadly, there is, and it is huge. As much as I will miss the former, I am truly excited to return to the latter. Goodbye to lost tombs, and hello again to libraries!*

# 36

I closed the book, and my eyes. I felt suddenly like I barely knew them – not just Mum and Dad, but Pan too. I had *loved* this past year. I'd never been so happy. I'd thought that was the same for the rest of my family. But it wasn't quite, I realized now. There was no question that they'd enjoyed parts of our missions, but they weren't there for the thrill. They were archaeologists and historians. They were there to preserve and protect history. I loved finding things; they loved what they were finding.

That was why the god had chosen me over any of them.

*Smash and grab.*

But I didn't know any other way. I wasn't a genius like the rest of my family. Libraries weren't for me. I had no way of saving them that *didn't* involve smash and grab, did I?

Unless...

I turned to the holosphere table. These devices usually used high-tech 7G networks, so this couldn't have been connected to the internet network in the house, which wasn't even fibre optic. My parents must have routed the system through a different network, which, I suspected, the People of the Snake weren't monitoring.

I reached to the screen, barely thinking, and tapped three precise points: my mum's passcode. She had never told me the code, but I'd seen her enter it into holospheres loads of times.

The screen crackled and came to life – projecting a single web page over the glass. It was blank, waiting for a command.

Should I do this?

Could I do this?

I had to try. I had to do *something*.

"Computer," I said, "look up Elena de Mosto, in Rome."

The white square flickered, and came back even brighter. A computerized voice spoke, causing the screen to pulse, as if it was talking: *"Located three Elena de Mostos in Rome, Italy."*

"*Professor* Elena de Mosto," I said.

Another flicker; the voice came back.

"Professor Elena de Mosto, professor of Roman history at the Capitoline Museums, Rome, Italy."

"That's the one," I said. "Intercept personal computer to send video message."

"Interception of personal devices is currently illegal according to—"

"Just do it anyway. Please."

The screen vanished, and for a moment I thought the holosphere had conked out – it had been sitting unused for over a year, after all. Now it returned, only this time rather than a white square, it projected an image of a sleepy-looking woman with a beehive pile of grey hair, squinting at me.

"Who is this?" she demanded. "How are you on my laptop?"

"Professor de Mosto," I replied, sitting up so she could see me better. "Please don't hang up. It's Jake Atlas. Do you remember me?"

Her eyes widened from squint to surprise. She slid her big, round glasses on, and leaned closer to her screen.

"*Mamma Mia*," she whispered.

"Professor, I need your help."

"My help? Do you recall what happened the last time you asked such a thing?"

Of course I did. Her museum ended up in ruins. No doubt hundreds of precious, priceless artefacts were destroyed. That had been my fault; I had told Mum to use the key to help us escape. I wouldn't have blamed this woman if she hung up on me straightaway and called the police. In fact, she probably should.

She took her glasses off and sighed. "Wait there," she said.

Then she walked off.

I waited for ten minutes, unsure if she would return. She'd left her computer on, so I was left staring at a blank, grey wall. I was about to turn away to read more of Mum's diaries, when she appeared again, sipping a tiny cup of coffee.

"Much better," she said. "It is really not worth talking to me before my morning espresso."

I mumbled an apology; I'd forgotten that it was only just past dawn in the UK, so early in Italy too. I'd woken the poor woman up, but she waved it away with a flap of a frail hand.

"First, tell me, are you all safe?" she asked.

What could I say? I needed her help, but I didn't want to get it by lying.

"No," I replied. "Professor, I don't know where my family are. I... I messed up. Things got bad. I mean, *really* bad."

"*Uffa!* Surely not worse than they were in Rome?"

"Much worse. You won't believe me if I tell you."

"But it sounds like you would *like* to tell me. As you know, I am an old lady, and very forgetful. I imagine I will not remember any of this conversation, should anyone ask."

She smiled and sipped her coffee. If she had been with me right then I would have hugged her. We already owed her so much. She was right, too: I did want to tell her. I felt so alone, and I needed to talk about what had happened. Maybe I could still fix it.

"Do you have time to listen?" I asked.

"All the time in the world. You may remember my office was recently destroyed."

"I'm sorry."

"I know, *signore*. Now, what is it you wish to tell me?"

"Some of it's going to sound weird."

"Some?"

"Well, all of it."

"I am prepared, young *signore*. I do not promise to believe all of what you say, but I will listen."

So I told her everything. I mean *everything*, from the very start, when my sister and I first discovered Mum and Dad were treasure hunters. It came pouring out in a breathless babble as I raced through the events of the past year. I told her about our missions to find the lost civilization's emerald tablets in Egypt, Honduras, China and Tibet. I told her about the incredible finds we had uncovered, and she gasped and muttered in astonishment. I told her how much of that archaeology had been destroyed, and she gasped again and turned a little pale. I told her about the People of the Snake, the black smoke, Morocco, Hadrian's Wall and the missing Ninth Legion, the promise to my dad that I had broken and the one I had made to my sister before she was taken. I told her about the keys, and my dreams of the door to which they needed to be returned to stop the god from becoming fully free and destroying the world.

It felt amazing to tell someone. The weight of it all had become unbearable. Telling Elena didn't suddenly make everything better, bring back any of the people I'd lost or change any of the stupid things I'd done; it just felt good not to be alone.

I expected her to say I had seen too many movies, or even to laugh at me. But she just smiled and listened. When I finally finished, she stared for several seconds, then rose from her chair.

"I need another coffee," she said.

Again she walked off. I waited several minutes, until she returned sipping from a much larger cup. "So, *signore*, what is it you wish from me?"

"I need your help."

"With what?"

"I have to find the door. That's the only way to stop the god, to save everyone."

"But what about your promise to your sister?"

"I ... have a plan for that. But I just need to find the door first."

"Well, if what you say is to be believed, there are people you can contact who will assist you in your search. Perhaps you can destroy more museums along the way."

I looked away, ashamed.

"I am sorry," she said, with a heavy sigh. "That was unfair."

"No, it was totally fair," I replied, and it was. "But that's not how I want to find the door. I want to do it the way my sister, and my parents, would want."

"How is that?"

I rubbed my eyes. I wasn't tired from the early start; in fact I felt more awake than I had in days. I was just barely able to believe what I was about to say.

"I want to study."

# 37

The next twelve hours were, well, not exactly normal for me. I used one of Mum's notebooks to write everything down. I knew that – if this all worked – my family would want to know precisely how we'd located the door.

*If.*

Elena said she'd join me in an hour. When she returned, she was sipping from an even bigger mug of coffee, as if each cup was training for the larger one to come.

"So, *signore*, where do we begin?" she asked.

I wasn't quite sure – thinking and studying weren't my specialities. Usually I just sat and listened as the rest of my family did all that.

"I've tried to think of what we know for sure about Marcus Turbo," I told Elena.

"Which is?"

"Two things. The date he became leader of the Praetorians and the date he vanished. It was between them that he found the door and the keys."

"So, the year 125 and, if your story is to be believed, the year 134. A nine-year period."

"But we also know that in that period Turbo visited Morocco and then Britain, where he disappeared. Let's say all that took roughly two years, so we can knock those off."

"Our timeline becomes the years 125 to 132. Seven years."

"OK. So in that period, Turbo led the Praetorians on a mission *somewhere*, to scout new land for riches. That's when he found the door and the keys. You agree?"

She considered it for a moment, and then nodded. "I agree."

Our next job was to look for any references to the Praetorian Guards in that period, so we got to work. For the next six hours, Elena searched though a mini-library she had at her home, while I scanned books and records on the holosphere, cross-referencing key words in the hope that I might hit on something. This time, though, we didn't get so lucky.

"There is nothing, *signore*. It is very strange. The Romans usually kept careful records of their military movements. Whatever missions the Praetorians were on between 125 and 132 they kept very secret."

In a way this was good news; if the Praetorians

had kept their movements secret, there was a reason. I rubbed my eyes, feeling tired for the first time all day. My stomach grumbled, and I realized it was past lunchtime and I hadn't even had breakfast.

"Perhaps we should take a break," Elena suggested. "We really cannot say where Turbo was in that time."

I looked up. "But could we say where he was before that?" I asked.

"Before? Yes, I think so. It would take some research."

I smiled my sweetest, most pleading smile. She sighed and nodded.

"Perhaps we should reconvene in another few hours? But only, *signore*, if you make me a promise?"

"What promise?"

"That you will eat something."

I kept that promise, at least, although I don't think Elena would have been pleased with my choice of lunch. I couldn't risk going outside in case I was spotted, so I raided the kitchen for any tins of food I'd missed the previous night. I had a starter of canned chickpeas, a tinned tuna main course and grapefruit segments for dessert. It wasn't exactly fine dining, but if Elena's research went well, I wouldn't have to live off year-old supplies for much longer.

I had a cold shower – there was no hot water – changed into some of my old clothes and rushed back to the chamber beneath the shed. I'd been trying to keep calm, but by the time I sat down again at the holosphere, I was buzzing all over, like I'd plugged myself into a power socket. I really felt like we could find the door, that we were close. We could save my family, maybe even save the world. I wondered if this was the same excitement that Pan had felt at Hadrian's Wall, solving the mystery of the Ninth Legion. I'd never be an academic like her, but I was beginning to understand the thrill. Historians were detectives, piecing together stories from tiny clues. In a weird way, it was fun.

That made it even more frustrating to sit waiting for another hour until the holosphere flickered back to life and Elena's face projected again from the screen.

"Ah, there you are," she exclaimed. "Have you eaten?"

"Lots," I assured her. "Did you find anything?"

"Also lots," she replied. "There are primary sources placing Marcus Turbo in several places in the years before our time slot."

"Hang on, I'll mark them on a map."

She waited as I instructed the holosphere to project a map of the Roman Empire and the regions beyond its borders around the time we'd specified. Then she insisted on checking the map and giving it her approval.

"Very good," she said. "So, before the year 125, Turbo commanded an army in Dacia."

"Dacia?"

"North of Greece, around Romania."

I highlighted the location on the hologram map with a glowing red dot. "Where else?"

"Well, from 113 he led an army in the Parthian campaign."

"The what?"

"Roman attempts to conquer Mesopotamia."

"Er...?"

"The area around Iraq today."

"Thanks. Is that all?"

"Not at all. Marcus Turbo was a very busy man. Fascinating, actually. I imagine he was a huge brute."

"Not really, he was quite short."

"Ah."

"Where else, then?"

"In 116 he put down a Jewish revolt in Judea. After that he was recalled to Rome, which is when he was made prefect of the Praetorian Guard, and our time slot begins."

"Great," I muttered, marking all the locations on the hologram map until there were five pulsing red dots around the Roman Empire.

"May I ask the point of that exercise?" Elena asked.

I nodded slowly, staring at the map. I wasn't entirely sure. I just had a hunch – one of my gut feelings.

"Other than Rome, these places are all on the borders of the empire," I said.

"Well, naturally. The army mainly operated on those borders, defending them."

"So it's possible that, at one of these places, Turbo heard of riches beyond the border. That maybe he returned there later, in our time slot, and went on the expedition that found the keys?"

"Well, that's speculation."

"But it's possible?"

"Yes, it's possible."

That was good enough for me – a chance. "OK, now look at where the Praetorians took the three keys. They knew they were dangerous, so they separated them and carried them as far from Rome as possible. Look at the three routes from Rome. To Morocco, Britain and the Black Sea."

On the hologram map I added red lines indicating the three voyages, although the routes were just guesses.

"Does that look right?" I asked.

"*About* right," Elena replied, not entirely convinced. "So, again, what is the point of all this?"

"Look at these routes, Professor. They go in three directions away from Rome. North to Britain, east to the Black Sea and west to Volubilis. But they *don't* go this way, south."

On the map I drew a blue line, showing the only direction that the Praetorians hadn't taken one of the keys: towards the Middle East and North Africa.

"Well, there were only three keys," Elena said. "So three routes."

"Yeah, that could be the reason. Or maybe it was

because Turbo didn't want to take any of the keys *back towards the door.*"

"Bah! More speculation, *signore.*"

"But, look, Professor. In that direction, south, there was one area that Turbo had visited before our time slot. This one here, the Meso-potty-place."

"Mesopotamia."

"Yeah, there. It's possible that while he was there Turbo heard tales of riches beyond the border. So he went back sometime after the year 125, to scout for a possible invasion location."

I was getting excited, talking faster, as I added another blue line tracing the route I was beginning to think Marcus Turbo and the Praetorians took to find the keys – and the door.

"He marched south, through Mesopotamia, until he hit this coast. Somewhere down here, on the Persian Gulf. This is it, Professor. Somewhere here is where he found the door."

"Why there? Why the coast?"

"Because the lost civilization was wiped out by a massive tsunami. Remember what my mum said about the similarities in the mythologies of Ancient Egypt, Sumeria, and other places? The mythical creators of those civilizations arrived on floodwaters. The lost civilization's homeland was destroyed by the god. It sank underwater. So we need to look at a sea, like here, the Persian Gulf. But part of their land survived. *That* was where the Romans found the door."

"So you mean an island close to the coast, in the Persian Gulf."

"Exactly! But it would be an unusual place, unlike anywhere Turbo had ever seen."

"Jake..."

"Professor, it would be a fragment of a lost world..."

*"Signore!"*

I'd been so lost in my rambling, staring at the map, I'd almost forgotten that Elena was watching me. "I'm sorry," I said. "But, Professor, I think this is it. I know it's still just speculation, and you won't agree, but if we study any islands off this coast, then maybe we'll find—"

"Why?"

"Eh?"

"I am curious, Jake. Why do you feel that you are so different to your sister, or your mother or father?"

"What?" I tried to hide my irritation at the question, which seemed to be moving away from the more important issue of finding the door. "I don't know."

"Of course you do. You think they are brighter than you. They are *academics*, while you are just the one who causes trouble. Am I correct?"

"Well, yeah, I guess."

"*Mamma mia*. What nonsense."

"What do you mean?"

"I mean, *signore*, that you have just solved an extremely puzzling historical mystery in..." She glanced down at her watch. "In thirteen hours. It seems to me that you are quite the equal of your sister. The equal, even, of your mother and father."

I smiled sadly. She was being nice, but I didn't believe it. Despite how desperate I was to save my family, I had actually enjoyed all of this history stuff, but only because it made me feel closer to Pan. I knew this for sure: she would have solved it way faster than me.

Actually, I hadn't solved anything. I was just guessing.

"We don't really know where the door is yet," I said. "Just a rough area, which we could—"

"Socotra."

"Eh?"

"Socotra," Elena repeated. "It is a small island in the Persian Gulf, and it fits your brief perfectly. I have heard that is quite unlike anywhere else on earth in terms of its flora. Indeed, those who have visited have reported that it looks like an alien planet."

Even as she was speaking, I instructed the holosphere to project images of the island. My arms prickled with goose bumps as I gazed at photos of a weird, unearthly landscape. Some of the trees looked like giant toadstools. Others were shaped more like massive turnips, with bulbous trunks and tiny sprouting branches. Ash-coloured mountains – huge mountains – plunged straight to a sea that was impossibly blue. It really did look like part of something much larger that had sunk into the ocean. A remnant of another land.

A lost land.

The images flickered, and I realized my hand was trembling on the holosphere screen. And not just my hand; I felt it all through me as I looked at Elena, then at the photographs, and back to Elena. The professor seemed troubled all of a sudden, and tired. She rubbed her eyes beneath her glasses and muttered something in Italian.

"Are you OK?" I asked.

"No, *signore*, I am very much not OK."

"You think this is all crazy, right?"

She sighed, so long and hard that her beehive hairdo swayed. "I once said that you are either crazy or you are on the verge of the greatest discovery in history. Now I wonder if perhaps both things are true."

She took a sip of what must have been her tenth coffee. It obviously had a calming effect, because when she set the cup down she was smiling again. Not exactly a "Whoo-hoo, we've cracked it!" sort of smile, but more the type of expression a teacher gives a hopeful student she knows is about to fail.

"Are you sure, Jake?" she said.

I realized that was the first time she'd used my actual name. She really was being serious.

"Well, I guess we can't be sure until the whole island's been searched," I replied, "and even then, maybe—"

"No," she interrupted. "I mean, are you sure you want to do this? You made a promise, do you remember?"

Of course I remembered. It hadn't left my mind for one second, not even during all the excitement of locating the door.

"I have a plan," I said. "I think it will work."

I considered that statement for a moment and then corrected it.

"It *has* to work."

# 38

I said goodbye to Elena and thanked her, promising that if things played out as I hoped they would – *prayed* they would – then we would visit her again in Rome, only this time to see the city properly, as tourists, not treasure hunters.

"As long as we're not still wanted international criminals," I'd assured her.

She lhad eaned closer to her computer's camera, took off her glasses and winked. "*Especially* if you are," she'd replied. "Now, after all that excitement I need another coffee. *Buona fortuna, signore!*"

I'd never felt as lonely, or as terrified, as I did in the few minutes after she hung up. My hand even moved to the holosphere screen as I considered calling again and making up some confusion over the location of the door. But I knew she'd see right through it. Over the past year, I'd trained myself not to look scared in the face of danger, even though I was usually petrified. I didn't want our enemies, mercenaries or rival hunters to see my fear, to use it against me. But had I called Elena back right then, I know it would have been written all over my face.

I slid my chair away from the holosphere screen, just in case I was tempted again to call the professor, and stared at the backpack that had been by my feet the whole time.

Finally, I had what I needed: the four keys and the location of the door. I wasn't stupid enough to think it would be plain sailing from here. Now that we had all four keys, there were two possible outcomes. We could use them to trap the god completely behind the door, and bring back all the people we had lost. Or they could be used to set the god fully free. I knew that Lord Osthwait was probably right: the god would try to use me to help it escape. It would get into my mind, trick me, threaten someone I love...

It would take everything I had to stop it. Maybe even *that* wouldn't be enough.

I sat for another few minutes staring at the bag, then picked it up and left the underground chamber.

My back ached from sitting down for so long, and my eyes were raw from tiredness and staring at the holosphere projections. My head throbbed too. Maybe that was the emotion of all of this taking its toll, or perhaps I just wasn't used to using my brain as much as I had over the past twelve hours.

There was no food left in the kitchen, other than some sugar and a tub of margarine. I ate a bit of each, drank some water and sat down again at the table, looking at the phone on the wall.

I was stalling.

I remembered a family dinner a few days before we went to Egypt, before Mum and Dad came out of retirement and I discovered their secret lives. It must have been on their mind that evening, going back to something they gave up over twelve years ago. Pan had sat across from me, doing her best to avoid talking to me, looking at me or acknowledging my presence in any way. Mum and Dad had chatted about their college lessons and asked us about school. Pan called her school a freak show and snapped at Dad for reminding her that she was there because she was so gifted and she should feel lucky.

"Lucky?" she'd seethed. Back then, she was always seething. "I'm not lucky to be a freak."

"Stop using that word, Pandora," Dad had insisted. "This is an amazing opportunity for you."

"Opportunity? For what?"

"To find something you love and do it properly."

"What thing? I don't love anything I do there."

Mum slammed her hand down on the table so hard that the cutlery jumped, and one of Pan's veggie sausages hopped off her plate and onto the floor.

"Then find something!" she barked. "Don't you dare waste what you have. For God's sake, Pandora!

Find what you love and do it and do it and knock yourself out doing it."

Pan and Dad and I sat staring, shocked and a little scared. Mum often snapped at us – we'd always deserved it – but not like that. It surprised her too. She was out of breath from the outburst, her face red.

"That's the only way you'll ever be happy," she added quietly.

We'd finished the meal in silence – you can't really go back to chit-chat after that – and later that night I'd heard Mum and Dad arguing in their room, although I couldn't make out the words because Pan had her music up so loud.

After that, after we'd gone to Egypt, everything happened so fast that I'd never really looked back to that evening. It hadn't seemed important. But a year or so later, Pan *had* found something she loved. Not all the charging around, smash-and-grab stuff, but the history and the archaeology. Sitting there without her, I sensed that my sister could grow up to become one of the most important archaeologists ever. I knew she would. I was so proud of her right then, and wished more than ever that she was with me. I'd have hugged her until she'd had to punch me to get free.

And what about me? I had found something that I loved too, even if Pan didn't approve. Studying with Elena had been exciting, but that wasn't me. I had a talent, and it wasn't best used in a library. Did that put me and Pan at odds? Did it have to?

Maybe not, if my plan worked.

*If.*

Again I considered picking up the phone and using Lord Osthwait's secret code to contact his organization. I could take the keys and travel with them to the door, and get my family back...

But I had made a promise.

I breathed in deeply, held my breath and let it go.

Then I rose from the table, picked up the phone and made the call.

*One-one-six-nine.*

I hung up.

I waited exactly three minutes.

I dialled again. *Two-two-seven-nine.*

The phone rang several times before someone picked up. The voice was crackly, deliberately distorted.

"Who is this?" it demanded.

"My name is Jake Atlas," I replied.

# 39

Have you ever seen a Hollywood movie in which the police track down some ultra-evil criminal mastermind and launch an all-out attack – swat teams, helicopters, sirens, loudspeakers bellowing warnings – the full works? Well, I'd kind of expected that. I'll be honest I'd hoped for it. It would have given the busybody neighbours something to talk about for decades.

In the end, though, the People of the Snake sent just one person, who simply rang the doorbell. I didn't hear it at first. I was upstairs listening to Pan's heavy metal music again, trying to puzzle out what about it she actually liked. I'd turned it up to almost full volume, expecting to hear the sirens and helicopters over the music, so it wasn't until the song changed and there was a temporary silence that I heard the doorbell buzzer.

I looked at my watch.

Seventeen minutes.

They were getting sloppy.

I turned off the music, picked up my backpack and went downstairs.

Actually, I stopped halfway down. Remember what I said about acting cool even when I'm terrified? Well, I'd never had to work so hard at it as at that moment. I gripped the stair handrail as the facade collapsed into sudden, full-on panic. My chest tightened, and a tremble rose though my body until I was shaking all over. I breathed in, but it didn't calm me. I breathed in again and again, deeper each time, as if I could somehow inhale courage from my home's dusty air.

"You made a promise," I whispered to myself. "You made a promise."

One last deep breath finally began to settle my heart – enough, I hoped, so that I could answer the door and look calm. I didn't let myself pause again to think. I continued down the stairs, unlocked the front door and opened it.

The first thing I noticed was that the front security light had not come on. Whoever had rung the bell had disabled it before approaching the house, which meant the visitor knew their stuff, which was promising. The person hadn't made the mistake of standing right by the door, either, in case of an ambush. Also good. Maybe this *was* do-able, I thought, as I squinted into the dark towards a lone figure standing in the shadows at the end of my drive.

In fact, I was the one being sloppy now. I was standing too far out in the open, where I could easily be taken out by a stun gun. As far as the People of the Snake knew, I might have been responsible for the disappearance of Lord Osthwait, Jessica and two dozen of their best mercenaries. To them, I was more dangerous than ever, and had I not remembered to speak at that moment, I'm sure I'd have felt the full force of an electrolaser bolt in my chest.

"I know the location of the door," I yelled, as quickly as I could.

The figure visibly flinched. A hand shot to an ear, and I heard a whispered command.

*"Stand down."*

The figure took one step closer, and called out – a woman's voice.

"Jake Atlas, you are surrounded."

Now *that* made me feel better. In all honesty, I was a little miffed about this one-person assault thing...

"Cool," I replied. "How many mercenaries? Hundreds, I bet? Can we just say hundreds, if my sister ever asks? She'll *freak*."

"Drop that bag and step forward with your hands in the air."

"No."

"Do it now or we will open fire!"

"Did you not hear me?" I called. "I know the

location of the door and I have all four keys, right here. I have everything we need to stop the god and get back the people we've lost. So do you want to waste more time with stupid threats, or do you want to talk? And stop acting like you've tracked me down. I called you, remember?"

Again, the woman's hand went to her ear to listen to a command. In the dark, I saw lights flicker on the lenses of her smart-goggles.

"What is it you want?" she asked.

"An army. To get this done. We'll need every single mercenary you have left."

"Agreed."

"And listen carefully; this is important. I want my family's criminal records wiped out. The police can announce that they made a mistake, or whatever. I know this isn't necessarily the end of this mission, so after this I want my Mum and Dad – Drs Jane and John Atlas – to be in charge of every operation for your organization. And my sister, Pan, will be your chief archaeological expert, your head of history, or whatever she decides. Pay them a *fortune*, too. I don't know how much. Whatever's a lot, then double it. Pan will give it all to animal charities, so think of it that way."

"What about you?" she asked.

"I'll work for them, doing what I do best."

"What is that?"

"Smash and grab."

"This is... This is highly irregular."

"Don't pretend this isn't what you wanted anyway. You'd have done anything to recruit us. Now you have, but on our terms. However my family wants to run things, they do it that way. *Properly*. Agreed?"

A long pause. More whispers in the dark. And then: "Agreed."

An engine started. A black van rolled silently out of the darkness down the street and stopped at the end of the drive. Its side door slid open, inviting me in.

"Are you ready then?" the figure asked. "We should go."

I breathed in. I really wanted to get in that van. Instead, I held the bag out at arm's length, for the person to come and take it.

"I'm not coming," I said.

"Excuse me?"

"I'm going to give you all the information you need, and you are going to bring my family back here, to our home. But I'm not coming with you, not this time."

"Uh... Hold on..."

I was still trying to look cool, but I couldn't help smiling as I heard more frantic whispering in the dark. The woman rushed to the van, and the whispers turned into a full-blown argument in a language I didn't know. Finally, the woman scuttled back to the driveway, out of breath from the squabble.

"You must come. It is non-negotiable."

"You're right," I agreed. "I'm not negotiating at all. I'm not coming."

"May I ask why?"

"No."

I didn't fancy telling them, and there wasn't time anyway – they had an apocalypse to stop, which was far more important that the weird emotions of a twelve-year-old kid. *I* knew why, and that was enough. I loved treasure hunting. But, first and foremost, I loved my family. I had made them a promise, and this time I was sticking to it.

There was a lot more squabbling, then the woman finally rushed forward to the doorstep and reached for my backpack. As she did, I caught a glimpse of her face in the half-light of the porch. She was a lot younger than I'd expected, and pretty too. There was something in her eyes that I recognized – steel. I was glad she was the one taking the keys.

"The location you need is written on a paper in here, along with the four keys," I explained.

She nodded and tried to take the bag, but I held on for a second.

"Bring them home," I said. "Please?"

"Yes, sir," she replied.

She took the bag, and then she was gone. The van roared off and I was left alone again.

# 40

I won't bore you with the details of the next four days. Mostly they involved me pacing the house or obsessively tidying in a failed effort to get my mind off what was or wasn't happening on a tiny island in the Persian Gulf. I went shopping for food, using money I found in Pan's piggy bank, and I wasn't arrested, so I guessed the People of the Snake had cleared our names. I watched the news a lot, scrutinizing every report about the Middle East, searching for any hint of what might be happening on Socotra Island. But I knew I wouldn't find one – the People of the Snake were too good.

I called Elena three times each day, babbling about what-ifs, and asking if I'd done the right thing. She kept assuring me I had, but I really didn't know. On the fourth day, I was making a tuna melt for dinner, when the doorbell buzzed.

I dropped the sandwich and ran to answer. As I got closer, I noticed that whoever was there had triggered the security light. I saw three shadows.

I burst into tears and threw open the door.

## ABOUT THE AUTHOR

Rob Lloyd Jones never wanted to be a writer when he grew up – he wanted to be Indiana Jones. So he studied Egyptology and archaeology and went on trips to faraway places. But all he found were interesting stories, so he decided to write them down. *Jake Atlas and the Keys of the Apocalypse* is Rob's sixth novel, although he has written over ninety other books for children, including non-fiction and adaptations of such classics as *Beowulf.*

About writing *Jake Atla*s, he says, "It began on a rainy day in the countryside. Stuck at home, I watched an Indiana Jones movie and then a Mission: Impossible film straight after. I wondered if you could mix the two: classic treasure hunts but with crazy high-tech gadgets. I especially wanted to set the first adventure in Egypt, a place and history that I'd loved so much since studying it at university. But I didn't really have a story, just an idea. Then, after becoming a dad, I realized that many parents are invisible in stories for young people. I decided to write about a whole family on an adventure together. But not just any family – one with troubles and squabbles, special skills and deep secrets..."

Rob lives in a crumbling cottage in Sussex, where he writes and runs and moans about mud.

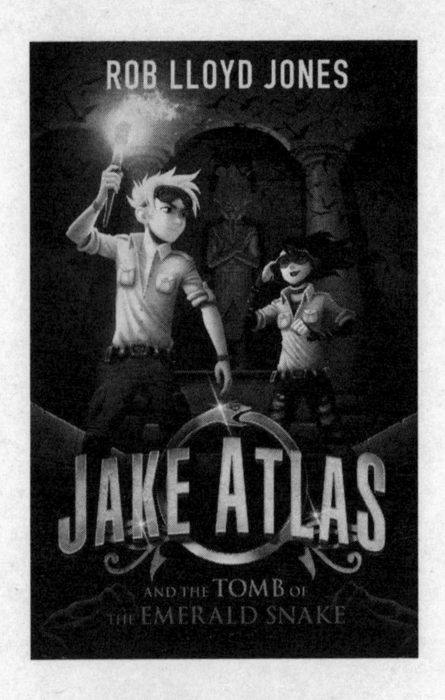


# JAKE ATLAS

## TOMB ROBBER, TREASURE HUNTER, TROUBLEMAKER

A couple of days ago I was a schoolboy with terrible grades and even worse behaviour – and a way of causing trouble that drove people nuts.

Now I am a member of a super high-tech treasure-hunting team searching for a lost tomb so I can save my parents from being turned into mummies by an evil cult.

Things have moved pretty fast...

# JAKE ATLAS

## TOMB ROBBER,
## TREASURE HUNTER,
## TROUBLEMAKER

Jake Atlas and his family are on the run.
They're on a mission to stop the mysterious
People of the Snake from hiding the
secret to the history of humankind.

But the international police are
chasing Jake and his family through
the jungles of Honduras – one of the
most dangerous places in the world.

The second thrilling Jake Atlas adventure.

# JAKE ATLAS

## TOMB ROBBER, TREASURE HUNTER, TROUBLEMAKER

Jake Atlas and his family may finally be close to discovering the secret history of humankind. Their quest takes them to Beijing and Tibet, then finally to the sacred Crystal Mountain.

But a mysterious savage creature guards the mountain, where untold dangers await.

As evil forces close in, this quest will push Jake harder than ever before.

The third thrilling Jake Atlas adventure.